A Second Chance

A Second Chance volume I, Volume 1

Edmond White

Published by Edmond White, 2017.

This is a work of fiction. Similarities to real people, places, or events are entirely coincidental.

A SECOND CHANCE

First edition. December 16, 2017.

Copyright © 2017 Edmond White.

ISBN: 979-8224514076

Written by Edmond White.

Table of Contents

A SECOND CHANCE PART 1

BY EDMOND WHITE

Text copyright @ Edmond White

All Rights Reserved

I praise God for giving me the talent to write. Without him, this wouldn't be possible. I would also like to thank everyone who has read my sample before the book was published. Your input, advice, and praises have been noteworthy. I hope my story touches your heart and inspires you in ways only you can imagine. It is the main reason why I continue pushing myself as a writer. I thank my son, mother, sister, and family for supporting me and my closest friends.

Last, I dedicate this book to my father, Edmond White Sr., Robert Harge Sr., Ms. Lucille Howard, and Mrs. Audrey Ayres. Gone, but always remembered. I will see you again one day.

Table of Contents

Prologue

Chapter 11- China

Prologue:

We turn our backs on God when there's good fortune flowing throughout our lives and search diligently for him in times of trouble. Men and women have become obsessed with individualism, and the need for instant gratification has taken over our thoughts and actions. We strive to become successful without concern for those less fortunate. Constant greed hinders us from understanding our true nature as human beings.

CHAPTER 1

PAUL

Bedford Mental Institution, New London Ct. November 2012

My name is Paul Mitchell the III. To my faithful parishioners, I'm Pastor Mitchell. I come from a generation of Southern Baptist ministers. Preaching is in my blood. My great-grandfather held the baton many years ago. He passed it along to my grandfather. My grandfather was able to give it to my father, and he handed it to me. The passing of the baton allows me to continue our religious journey. Each of them firmly believed in their faith, whereas my faith has taken a devastating turn. The recent change in my life has led me to attempt suicide. Growing up as a preacher's child is a monumental task within itself. The same rules given to my peers didn't apply to me. My father's instructions were to carry myself like a child of God wherever I traveled. I had my struggles just like any other teenager. I did what my father asked of me, although it took some time to understand thoroughly. As the years passed, I became a model son and a great minister. My church is continually expanding. It's currently two thousand members strong.

The ministers I'm familiar with have said God had spoken to them at some point in their lives. They specified this overwhelming experience or calling catapulted their decision to become ministers. God has never talked to me directly, but I can feel his remarkable presence whenever I enter the pulpit. The driving force behind my decision to preach was my father. Everyone says I'm a spitting image of him. He stood a handsome six-foot-two. My father was two inches taller than me, with light brown eyes and a creamy buttermilk complexion. I enjoyed

watching him address the congregation during my youth. He delivered his sermons so eloquently. My father made believers out of individuals who had never attended church before hearing his message.

He saved many souls from despair. I've heard countless stories of how my father would go out of his way to help a troubled person in need. Black folks from all walks of life would hover around his back porch in long lines to receive clothing, food, and sometimes money if they could not afford rent. My father felt contented when he helped someone.

He thought it was our duty to give to those in need. His gift of giving went well beyond the neighborhood. He also traveled abroad to other countries and volunteered to give back to societies in dire straits. My father influenced me greatly. I'm just an old-fashioned Baptist preacher. I have no power except in the words I speak. The spirits of my parishioners become empowered when they hear my influential message. I've also saved numerous individuals from the pitfalls of life. I frequently pray for the sick at hospitals. I often visit the juvenile detention centers, speaking to troubled youth. I'm in various organizations for the uplift of the community. My plate is complete, but I enjoy every moment of serving those who need guidance. *I can help everyone escape their demons but not elude my own.*

CHAPTER 2

CHINA

Greenwich, Connecticut

China Reynolds brushes her thick, light brown hair fifty strokes daily. She read the information from Cosmopolitan magazine on how to manage your hair. China methodically starts at the tip of her roots, sliding the pink brush with black thistles past her uneven ends. She desperately needs a haircut and thinks a few inches off her hair will be sufficient. The loud vibration from her cell phone lying against the dresser disrupts her strokes. Annoyed, she stops at number thirty-nine. Glancing at her phone, she notices her mother's number. She takes her time before answering it. Today is Sunday. China knows her mother will ask her the same vexing question she asks every Sunday morning. China is not in the mood to argue. She is enjoying her quiet Sunday. She touches her iPhone, hesitating briefly before speaking.

"Hello," she barely says.

"Are you coming to church today?" *The ill-reputed question is sickening to China.* She loves her mother even though they have an unsteady relationship. Henrietta raised China alone. Her father left the home when she was just a baby. There are no memories of him or any pictures for China to see. Henrietta discarded his belongings when he moved into another woman's house. She's

never spoken about him and hasn't been with anyone since. That was thirty years ago. After the devastating breakup, she dedicates herself to God only. Henrietta attends church five times a week, carrying a black King James Bible and wearing a silver chain connected to a silver cross

around her neck. She preaches the word of God to anyone who cares to listen; she will even preach if you don't want to hear it.

"I told you when I'm ready, I will call you," she answers, agitated.

"Chile!" She hates it when her mother calls her that.

"What if something happens to you tomorrow? You will not have enough time to get ready. Jesus is coming back like a thief in the night. Chile, you need to get yourself ready for his return." China sets the phone on speaker. She doesn't have time to sit there holding her phone and arguing with her mother.

"Are you still there, China?"

"I'm still here, Mom," she says, wishing she was elsewhere.

"What you gonna do?"

"You call me every Sunday morning asking the same thing. My answer hasn't changed. I'm not ready to commit myself to church. Church is the last thing on my list right now. I have a lot of things to take care of first."

"Last on your list?" You're putting God last?" Henrietta questions at the top of her lungs. "No, Mother," she detects frustration in China's voice.

"Well, that's what you said, isn't it?"

"You know what I mean."

"I don't know what you mean. I raised you in the church since you were a baby. You know God. So why are you acting like you don't?" China remains silent, counting her last strokes. *She figures why bother trying. It's Henrietta's way or nothing at all.*

"China?" She doesn't respond. "China, do you hear me?" Henrietta yells through the phone. China ignores her.

"Mother, I have to go. Bye." China taps into a number on her cell phone, and her hairstylist answers.

"I need you, A.S.A.P. "

"I'll be there in an hour."

CHAPTER 3

DAVID

Percival Molson Stadium, Montreal, Canada

David Parks rushes past the thirty-yard line. He sees the end zone, knowing he will score a touchdown. David weighs two hundred twenty-five pounds. He's five feet eleven inches and built like a fine-tuned machine. The Associated Press named him the fastest running back in the Canadian Football League. He runs a four-forty slightly under four seconds. A cornerback from the opposing team manages to get close, but David's speed is no match for the defensive player. David pulls away as if the corner's standing still. He crosses the goal line. The referee throws both arms up, signaling a touchdown as the fans roar inside the sold-out stadium.

David worked diligently over the years to improve himself. He attended a small Division II School in North Carolina. Alms College is known for its academics. The athletic program seemed nonexistent once David arrived. His record-breaking runs and numerous touchdowns received full media attention, enabling him an opportunity to turn pro. His family supports him. His friends envy him, and the CFL fans adore him. There is only one thing missing. He has no one special to share his accomplishments with. Women infuriate David. As an adolescent, he discovered their true intentions, keeping a steady guard for their hidden agenda. He finds the opposite sex attractive, but he doesn't trust them. Most women approach David because of his celebrity status. Over time, he realized his money and fame meant more to them than anything else, so he avoided women most of the time. David and his teammate Cedric Thomas are drinking inside Ray's café. It's a local bar adjacent to the football stadium.

"Dave, you were on your game today. I've never seen you run like you ran today. You were a blur even in slow motion," Cedric declares, sipping his Heineken.

"I felt invincible today. The front line gave me a lot of open spaces. I have to take those guys out to dinner. I owe them the world. They make a brother look real good."

"How long has it been?" Cedric asks, eyeballing the cute waitress walking past their table. "How long for what?"

"You know, since you had a steady woman," David sighs.

"You're on that again?"

"All I'm saying is that you need a nice lady in your life, someone to come home to every night like Samantha. Samantha and I have been married for five years. She's my soul mate," David gives him a twisted look.

"If she's your soul mate, why are your eyes following that waitress around the room?" Cedric takes another sip of beer, removing his droopy eyes from the waitress.

"It's no harm in looking, David. My eyes might roam a bit, but my heart belongs to Samantha. I've never cheated on Samantha."

"So if she came here and asked you to sleep with her, you wouldn't?"

"I'm a married man, Dave. I respect my wife. I cherish what we have."

"It doesn't seem like you're respecting her now."

"We all look, David, both men and women," Cedric changes the subject.

"I want you to meet someone."

"Cedric, every time I talk with you, there's a new woman for me. I'm not interested. I'm tired of dating the same type of females."

"Please hear me out first. You need a woman. People are starting to think you're gay." "What people?"

"Your fans and the media. The rumors are spreading fast."

"They can think what they want. I'm not gay. I've been on countless dates with women who do nothing for me. All they want is to look good and live off my name."

"A few NFL teams are looking to sign you, which will lead to a sizable pay grade. When it happens, you will need a woman in your corner to help you grow, so you must find a true person who won't steal from you like these groupies."

"Is this a marriage arrangement? You know you're something else. I haven't met this woman, and you're already planning my future?"

"It's not like that. Trust me."
"Then what is it like? Explain it to me," his expression turns serious.

"I'm telling you, David, this woman is special. If I weren't married, I would take her for myself," David laughs.

"Are you for real?" Cedric nods, smiling, revealing the gap between his front teeth. "I'm for real. I have a picture that will make you change your mind."

"I doubt it," Cedric takes out his brown leather wallet that looks like it's been through a war.

"That old thing is falling apart. I would be embarrassed to carry that around," David shakes his head in disgust.

"It serves its purpose. My wallet and I have spent many years together," Cedric carefully pulls out the picture, holding onto it like the winning Powerball ticket. He then licks his lips.

"Mm, mmm, mmm, she is one fine sister. If you don't take her, I might file for a divorce," he says jokingly.

"Do you know how many pictures of women I've seen? It won't change a thing. If you've seen one, you've seen them all, and I've seen my share. Trust me."

"I bet you haven't seen this one. Just look at the picture," Cedric demands. "For what? It's just a waste of time."

"I'm telling you, once you see this picture, you'll change your mind."

"Put the picture on the table face down, Cedric."

"Face down? I don't get it."

"I like suspense and the thrill of not knowing if she looks the way you say she does. She can be ugly for all I know."

"I have good taste, and you know it. The women I've dated have always looked the best," he says proudly, sticking out his chest. Cedric places the picture face down and then nudges it across the table.

"I'll take little peeks at it until I can see the entire picture."

"You always have to make things difficult," Cedric groans, showing his displeasure. *David peels back a corner of the picture, revealing the woman's face. He looks at her face and can't believe how beautiful she is.*

"Wow! Where did you find her?" Cedric sucks his teeth.

"Now, do you believe me? My wife hangs out with her from time to time, and the kicker is she's single."

"Tell her it's a date."

"Are you serious, David? Don't make me set this up for you to back out at the last minute." "Have I ever lied to you?"

"No."

"Well, set it up then."

CHAPTER 4

Bedford Mental Institution

Sitting here in this foreign room, I realize I don't belong. I'm not crazy, but many would disagree. I can hear the wind gusting alongside the window behind me. The cold New London Ct air entices my neck from a slight draft seeping through the confined window. The relaxing environmental purpose is to change the abnormal to normal. I'm sitting inside the visitor's room, eavesdropping on conversations of family members talking with their loved ones. The room has eight lengthy tables with two in each row and four chairs on both sides to accommodate visitors. It resembles a cafeteria, but it's smaller in size. A black refrigerator with a long silver handle is next to a white tabletop counter in the far right-hand corner. The fridge holds snacks, and a chrome coffee maker sits on the countertop. The fresh smell of charcoal gray paint lingers inside. Contemporary Halogen lights extend from a high ceiling, exhibiting brightness to an unclear situation for many of us.

Bryson Jennings and his mother are in a passionate conversation next to me. Bryson is Asian-part Irish, and he has boyish gray eyes. Dressed in a brown robe and slippers, Bryson cries to his mother to get him released. He expresses he's lonely and misses his friends. His mother has identical gray eyes to Bryson and speaks broken English. She's a little heavy and continues to shed tears along with him. She removes her three-quarter-length black wool coat and places it behind her chair, then comforts his pain by embracing him. When they disengage, she tells him he must stay longer than expected. The unpleasant news breaks his spirit. Bryson has Paranoid Schizophrenia. Someone brought him here because he decided to burn a woman's house down for speaking badly about him. Bryson accuses everyone of spreading lies. He thinks the entire world is against him. There is also an older man named Harold Minor in the far corner by the refrigerator, chatting with his wife. He has white hair, beige skin, velvety black eyes, and a nasty expression. Harold hasn't changed his attire since my arrival. He is wearing his favorite blue denim Lee jeans and a white cardigan sweater matching his not-so-white slippers.

His wife, an attractive-looking black woman with short black hair and honey-brown eyes, pleads with him to listen. She tells him he will be able to go home soon and not to worry about things at home. He yells back at her, cursing the day he was born. Her eyes fill with tears as she covers his hands with hers. Our New London, Connecticut experience differs from the inhabitants who dwell here and the visitors looking for a delightful time. We are miles away from New London's waterfront district, which captures the imaginings of its citizens. The winter nightlife in New London is a fun time for people in this area.

The twenty-six-block district combines art, music, design venues, one-of-a-kind boutiques, and thirty eateries. Tourists travel the timbered community by ferry, bus, and train. I-95 North is often congested with cars heading further out to Foxwoods Casino. It's a swell time for those looking for excitement, but the pleasures evade us residing in this place. I arrived at Bedford Mental Institution five months ago. Bedford rests upon an immense rocky landscape. Its bright red brick building leans right, facing a vast wooded area due to its uneven foundation. Green undergrowth and a foul odorous muck inhabit the wooded area. A ten-foot barbed wire fence surrounds the college dormitory architectural structure. It has six brick pillars supporting the building at every angle. Window-size steel cages prevent the unwanted from escaping. Bedford has three floors separating its patients. I occupy the first floor with patients considered less of a threat to themselves and others. Monitored more closely are the second-floor patients. Heavily medicated patients are assigned to the third floor, ensuring their aggressive behavior does not become a problem for staff and others. Visitors are buzzed in through two steel doors when entering Bedford Mental Institution. The doors are always locked, keeping society safe from its outcasts. A petite white woman named Francine with a crew cut-styled spiked blond haircut sits as the gatekeeper, allowing those with proper authorization to enter.

I eagerly observe the steel doors from the visitor's room, hoping the gatekeeper will brighten my day. My family has disowned me. The church has turned its back on me; the public wants my head. My mother refuses to talk to me, saying a man of God should have known better. No one comes to visit. I haven't seen my sister, and she's the only person who truly understands me. After the murder of my father on my eighteenth birthday, she became my crutch. I blame myself for my father's death. He died when an intruder broke into our home, killing him. It happened when I was out celebrating. I was out drinking, smoking, and acting like a buffoon. These are the exact words my father reiterated to me when he was alive. I should've spent more time talking with him and sharing those critical father-and-son moments I let him escape. My ambition prevented me from seeing the truth. I never fully understood what he wanted out of me. If I had, then maybe he would still be alive today. S

Sharon cared for me as I mourned my father's passing. She acts more like a mother than an older sister. She aided me in diverting the constant dangers in my life. Sharon provided tough love, not ever holding back any punches. At all times, she was painstakingly candid. She instructed me to act like a man and to put away children's things. Her tough love allowed me to

change my route as a teen. I was born down a dead-end street with nowhere to turn. It hurts not to feel her presence in this God-forsaken building. *Visiting hours are almost over. Loved ones are beginning to leave, and the gatekeeper will soon retire, ending my anticipation.*

CHAPTER 5

Concert Hall, Cleveland, Ohio

China critiques her hair in the dressing room mirror. She decided to try a new hairstyle. Her auburn peekaboo bob cut radiates. She is highly pleased with the work of her hairstylist. Her dressing room door opens.

"Are you ready to take the stage?" Her manager asks.

"I certainly am," China answers with confidence.

"Well, your fans await you."

"Give me a few minutes."

"Ok, you got it."

Singing is her life. As a child, her voice excelled above the rest. She sounded more like a woman than an eight-year-old. The first time she performed onstage at the Apollo Theatre, China reached notes, captivating the audience. Her breathtaking performance allowed her to win the first-place prize of one thousand dollars. China earned ten thousand dollars after winning ten consecutive weeks before losing to a homeless man telling jokes. Her stardom started early in life. At the tender age of thirty-three, her followers continue to be in awe, just as they were when she was a child. China peers out from behind the curtain. "Come Love Me," her latest single, has been steady, holding the billboard charts at number one for five solid weeks, showing no indication of letting up. Excitement fills the sold-out arena. The twenty-three thousand plus fans eagerly shout her name. China feels secure. Her fans provide a security blanket and a relentless love she never experienced from her father.

As China scans the stadium, she can't help but envy the enthusiastic daughters escorted by their fathers. She considers how fortunate they are to have a dad in their life. China stands behind the curtain and recalls a moment in life that made her despise her mother. When China's dad left home, her mother developed alcoholism before traveling on her sanctified journey. She started casually drinking. One afternoon, when China was ten, somebody revealed something significant to her. Upon helping her mother clean the house, she discovered an old picture of her mom and dad hidden underneath paper clutter inside Henrietta's dresser drawer. Henrietta looked joyful and carefree and didn't appear to worry about the world.

Back then, her brown hair was long, thick, and healthy. Her figure was enticing. Her brown eyes seemed happy, and her dad looked very handsome in the photo, with eyes identical to those of China. They were embracing each other while smiling for the camera. China desires to clutch the picture forever and be a part of her mom and dad's happiness. Unexpectedly, her mother walks in behind her, snatching the image.

"Mom, I know that's my father. Why won't you let me see him?" She pleads.

"He's not your father. Your father left us a long time ago. It takes more than a sperm donor to be a father. My husband ran off with someone else. He belongs to another woman now. I'm your mother and your father. Do you understand me, China? I'm your mother and your father," she yells, grabbing China firmly by the arm and pulling her closer. China tries to pull away. Her mother squeezes her arm tighter.

"You're hurting me."
"Stay still, Chile, before you make me lose my patience."

"It's not fair, mom. All of my friends have fathers. Why can't I?" She cries. China squirms to free herself. After listening to her emotional plea, Henrietta lets go of her. China's pain impacts the agony in her own heart as well. Henrietta touches China's face.

"That's just the way it is, young girl. He doesn't want you, and he doesn't want me. He would rather live with someone else and care for their family. One day, you'll understand. Some things we have no control over."

"He may not want you, but I know my daddy wants me," her comment infuriates Henrietta. She slaps China's face.

"Don't you ever come out of your mouth like that again, girl? You respect me. I'm the one raising you, feeding you, and clothing you. If it weren't for me, you would be homeless. Your father sure doesn't give a damn about you!"

"You can change it, Mom, by letting me see him," China wipes her face.

"I said no. End of discussion. Do I make myself clear?"

"Yes, Mom, I understand."

"Now go to your room," her heart is filled with pain and disappointment. China lowers her eyes and reluctantly departs without the picture.

The picture conjures up memories Henrietta assumed were suppressed. *She remembers the scenery like it was yesterday. It was a warm sunny day in July and marked their first date. The two chose to picnic in Evergreen Park, eventually leading to their first kiss. She kindly asked a Caucasian man in the park to photograph them. Henrietta suddenly visualizes the moment and becomes distressed, with every thought running rapidly throughout her mind. Her heart longs for William.* She drops to her knees and begins to break down. After that, she settles in a deep depression. She chops off her hair, and her drinking binges are more noticeable to those around her.

She neglects China and often leaves her alone at home while visiting the neighborhood bar. Upon her departure, Henrietta tells

China not to open the door for anyone. She will return shortly. Her mother habitually returns to the home at unreasonable night hours, leaving China alone several times. Many nights, a fearful China curls herself up in the closet, waiting for her mother to return. China can always detect when her mother is taking off. Henrietta will treat her to McDonald's and buy her a new toy before leaving. As time passes on, China discovers things to keep her occupied. China dresses in her mother's clothing. She wears makeup, pretending to be a beautiful woman instead of an eight-year-old child. She finds empty vodka bottles around the house, imitating her mother's drunken manner.

The fascination that entirely draws her attention is the late-night music videos. BET alters China's dreadful world. The artists express their circumstances through song and dance. When happy, the artists sing about joyous times, showing joyful moments. And when sad, the artists sing about pain, filming it also. Their clothes are trendy, and their bodies are perfect. China desires to be exactly like them. She mimics their style, expression, and soothing vocals. She imitates their dance moves, learning to move gracefully with each step. Maria Carey, Mary J Blige, and Janet Jackson became her surrogate mothers. She promises herself one day, she will receive love from the world as they have. When China walks out on stage, she feels the love from adulated fans. *The night is perfect except for the weird tingling sensation in her lower back.*

CHAPTER 6

David has been dating Cathy Emerson for a month. The blind date was a huge success. He's never met anyone like her. Cathy looks stunning in her figure-hugging red dress. Her striking, pleasant features are more than David can handle. He finds it incredibly hard to keep his eyes off of her. David and Cathy sit across from each other inside Barclay's restaurant. It's a high-class spot in Montreal, Canada. The restaurant's inside arrangement emulates a football field. Green artificial turf ornaments on the floor display white yard line numbers under every table.

Dressed as a coach is the hostess, and the waiters and waitresses in referee attire. Separated by a glass partition, the dome ceiling opens to let in sunlight during the day and moonlight in the evening. The food is delicious, and the service is impeccable. Many prominent names and celebrities attend the place often. When David and Cathy enter the restaurant, she receives most of the attention from the other patrons.

"David, do you know that a person's eyes are a pathway to their soul?"

"What did you say?"

"Didn't you hear me, David?" She breaks his trance.

"I'm sorry. Can you repeat it?"

"A person's eyes are a pathway to their soul."

"Oh, I never knew that."

"Like your eyes, for example."

"What about my eyes?" He weakly asks.

"Your eyes tell me a lot about your soul."

"They do?" Again, his attention drifts away from the conversation as he stares at her beautiful features.

"You have strong, unwavering brown eyes. I can tell your soul is full of power. You can do anything if put to the test. What do you think?" David doesn't reply.

"Earth to David, did you land yet?"
"I'm sorry Cathy, I... had a moment."

"Can you please share your important moment with me because you are not listening to me at all, and it's kind of annoying?" She questions, a tad bit irritated.

"Every day that passes, my feelings grow more for you. Please don't take this the wrong way what I'm about to say. Women approach me constantly because of my profession. I've turned down a lot of offers. I'm not a dog. I'm not conceited. I respect the opposite sex, but when I first saw your picture, it set off so many emotions," her face stiffens.

"Um, hum, I bet. Is this emotion sexual by any chance?" She asks derisively. "I know it's been a month of abstinence, but I believe in marriage first," she probes his mannerisms for the truth.

"No, no, it's nothing like that. I don't care about the sex. I can't describe it, but you complete me," David caresses Cathy's hands.

"That's so sweet. I feel the same way about you," she leans over the table, sticking out her lips. David presses his lips firmly against hers.

"So, what do you think?"
"About what?"
"Your soul, silly."
"I've never really thought about it like that."
"Do you attend church?"
"No."
"Have you ever attended church?"
"No, church isn't my thing," Cathy frowns.

"Do you believe in God?"

"I can't say that I do. I don't believe in the Bible. I think it's men looking for credit. The stories are like fantasy, similar to Greek mythology," his words sound offensive. Her warm eyes turn icy cold.

"How can you say that?" She raises her voice and draws attention from the other couples dining in the restaurant. "God is real. I'm a true believer. He's done so much for me. I never miss a Sunday at church. You need to wake up David," she shakes her head judgmentally.

"What are you talking about?"

"I knew it was too good to be true," the corners of her mouth turn downward. "I don't understand."

"Our relationship and everything seemed so perfect, but I can't continue this relationship if you don't believe in God. He means everything to me," David closes his eyes, pondering it. *He likes Cathy, but no one will make him believe in a God that doesn't exist.*

"Well, it is what it is," David walks out of the restaurant.

CHAPTER 7

Bedford Mental Institution

Another couple of days have passed, and still no visitor. By now, I'm used to it. I spot Alex hugging and then kissing her mother on the cheek. Her mother whispers something in her ear before departing for the steel doors. After her mother exits, she decides to join my empty table.

"Paul, I can't believe no one has stepped through these doors after five months to see you. You've helped so many people when their backs were against the wall. Why aren't they here to support you? How can they call themselves true Christians and be so unforgiving?"

"Alex, there's nothing I can do about it. I can only keep praying, asking God to take care of me. Men and women will deceive you every time, but God will never forsake you."

"But it's so wrong, Paul. You don't deserve this treatment. A lot of us in here are crazy. I don't think you're one of us, though. You seem very normal to me," I laugh at her amusing statement.

"Well, thank you so much, Alex. I appreciate your generosity, especially at a time like this, but the state of Connecticut has labeled me the same as everyone else inside these walls. I'm no different."

Alexandria Poretti is a long-term patient at the psychiatric center. Everyone calls her Alex. Everyone calls her Alex because she dresses more like a man than a woman. Underneath the

Mets baseball hat, blue hoody, and sagging white sweatpants lie a beautiful, voluptuous Italian woman with mysterious dark eyes.

"Have you seen the doctor today?" She asks, tucking a strand of hair inside her hat. "Not yet, but I'm sure he will be here soon to question me all over again."

"Why must he frustrate us so much? He asks many questions and doesn't believe us when we answer them. I can't stand him, especially the way he stares at me. His enormous eyes remind me of a bullfrog. He's creepy-looking, and he makes my skin crawl. Yuck! I try to avoid him at all costs," I agree with her about his exterior. The doctor will never win a modeling contest.

"I guess he's our last chance of getting out of this place. His word is the final say." "I'll never make it out of this place."

"Hey, no negative talk. You have to believe you'll get better. You must show the doctor you're ready to leave this place for good."

"And how must I do that? He makes me very uncomfortable. I freeze up in my therapy sessions. I can feel his eyes undressing me, so I sit there, unable to explain to him that I'm better now."

"In all my therapy sessions, I'm facing the opposite way toward the wall. How is it that you can feel his eyes on you?" Exasperated, she stares at me, sulking.

"In every therapy session I've had so far, I'm always directly in front of him. He sits an arm's length away from me," I shake my head in disbelief.

"The next time you're with him, ask to face the wall so you can concentrate," she pulled down her hat, covering her eyes to avoid showing her true feelings.

"What if he doesn't let me?"

"Then close your eyes and do not open them until you stop talking. Stay focused, and don't let the doctor distract you. Can you do this, Alex?" She nods her head in agreement. Her dark eyes almost seem to brighten.

"Yes, I can do it, Paul. I'm getting out of here before they torture me."

"Before they torture you? What are you talking about?"

"The doctor and his demented staff," I sense fear in her voice.

"The torturing of mentally ill patients doesn't exist anymore. It's illegal. We have rights." "It's still going on," she whispers, careful not to be heard.

"Trust me, Alex. It isn't true," I try to reassure her.

"Then why do I hear screams from my room in the middle of the night?"

"It's probably someone having nightmares. This place will certainly do it for you. I've had some myself.

"No, that's not it. Underneath my room, I can hear men screaming through the heating vent. I can hear the doctor's laughter. It's frightening, and I can't even fall asleep some nights. The screams play throughout my head," she checks the room to see if anyone is listening.

"Relax, Alex, because I'm sure there's a legitimate explanation. The torturing of patients is unlikely. We are living in the twentieth century. The screams must be coming from something else," she disagrees. Unsatisfied with my reasoning, she decided to stop talking about it.

"I will try to do better in my therapy sessions so I can leave this institution," she says, redirecting the conversation with doubt in her eyes.

"That's what I'm talking about, Alex, a little confidence and lots of praying."

"Paul, can you promise me something?" She removes her hat, letting her jet-black hair fall against her shoulders. Her mood turns sensual. Our eyes link together.

"Yes, what would you like me to promise?"

"When you leave this place, please take me with you?"

"Certainly, Alex, it's already done," we shake hands. She walks off to her room.

Alex is the only person with whom I've shared my true feelings other than the doctor. She was the first person to greet me when I arrived. Alex has made my stay more manageable. Her knowledge of Bedford has been immeasurable. Bedford has been her home for over a year. The staff keeps a close eye on her. I think the gatekeeper and team desire her. Maurice, Curtis, and Ricky are their names. We call them the good, the bad, and the ugly. Maurice is a supportive staff member. He's there for us whenever we need help. If you're feeling down, Maurice will talk to you.

If you have questions, he will answer them; if you need advice, he will give his input. On the other hand, Curtis makes our stay at Bedford as miserable as possible. He bashes most of the patients with constant verbal assault. Many of us have a hard time handling his insults, especially Harold. On two separate incidents, Harold nearly lost it. He threatened to break Curtis's neck if he didn't stop the name-calling. Staff had to quickly intervene to prevent Harold from actually doing it. Curtis lacks people-person skills. If you need help, he refuses and calls you weak. If you have questions, he ignores you and tells you to ask someone else; if you need advice, he will say he's not a doctor. The problem with Ricky has to do with his appearance and personal hygiene. His face is hurt, and no one wants to look at him. He smells awful, and we turn the other way, holding our noses whenever he comes around. He does have a good quality, though. He cares. He particularly cares for Alex. I often see staff whispering to each other whenever she enters the room and gawking at her like a piece of meat. Francine and Ricky give me dirty looks whenever Alex is near me. If looks could kill, six feet under is where I would be.

I believe Alex can feel their lustful eyes burning a hole through her body, but she ignores them. Her stay here has been more extended than that of most patients. She has attempted suicide on ten different occasions. Her attempts range from slitting her wrists, swallowing a bottle of sleeping pills, jumping in front of a moving city bus, and trying to hang herself with a noose. Each time she tried, someone was there to save her. I told her it was not her time yet. *God has something in store for her. I guess he has something in store for me as well.*

CHAPTER 8

CHINA

Greenwich, Connecticut

The doctor's words are not what China wants to hear. Over the past several weeks, the numbness in her lower back remains. She feels weak. Her vision is impaired, and her coordination is diminishing. Standing for extended periods is growing difficult. Ninety percent of China's salary requires performing on stage and interacting with her fans. China's staff carried her to her dressing room at the end of her last concert. China informed everyone she needed a rest. She's toured five cities in eight days.

"Kelly, I need a few days to recuperate," China says, lying in bed.
"Are you sure a few days are enough?"
"I should be ok after a few days off my feet."

"I can get you more time. How about a week instead? I can postpone some of your tour dates."
"I can't disappoint my loyal fans. They need me, and I need them. My fans have stayed the course when everyone else hasn't," Kelly looks concerned. *How can she explain to China her loyal fans are growing impatient? Her last performance was dreadful. At one point on stage, china forgot the lyrics to her song, causing a chorus of boos from the audience. China was a great dancer as a teen, but her recent dance routines lacked rhythm and organization. China appears lost, and no one can figure out why.*

"You get some rest. I will call you in a few days."
"Thanks, Kelly. I need it."

"My job is to make sure you can perform at your best. I will take care of everything. Don't you worry about a thing?"

Talent has surrounded Kelly Anderson her entire life. As manager of various artists, she has seen her share of great performers come and go. She knows when they're at the top of their game and recognizes when father time has set in. Their vocals are the first to diminish from years of strain and failure to care for their vocal cords. As the artists increasingly age, their performances suffer,

which causes a landslide in ticket sales, furthering the big-name arenas' loss of interest fast. China is far from that point in her career. She has plenty of fuel left in her tank. Shortly after Kelly leaves China's luxurious home in Greenwich, Connecticut, warm tears saturate China's face. The doctor's prognosis replays over and over in her head. *"You have Multiple Sclerosis."*

CHAPTER 9

DAVID

David has a legitimate reason for not believing in God. When David turned five, he lost both parents in a car accident. David managed to survive the harrowing ordeal. His father's SUV turned over several times on the highway, ejecting both parents and killing them instantly. When paramedics arrived, David sat in his car seat unharmed without a scratch. Witnesses described it as a miracle, saying God was saving him for something. When David lost his parents, a vicious custody battle ensued between both families. His mother's Caucasian family and his dad's African-American family detest one another.

David's white family doesn't believe his dad's family can take care of him. His white grandmother complained of how "ghetto" they were. She claims they lack education, live in poor living conditions, and do not have the proper resources to raise David. The court agreed with David's grandmother, awarding her full custody. Through court stipulations, David can stay with his dad's family every other weekend. Some of his fondest memories were spending time with Uncle Chuck, his dad's younger brother. Uncle Chuck looks older than he appears, and his mouth sinks slightly from missing teeth. Uncle Chuck is thirty-five years old, ten years younger than David's deceased father. He has a stocky build, piercing black eyes, and a rugged cinnamon face as hard as nails. Chuck teaches him things David will never learn in the squeaky-clean suburbs. He understands how to defend himself by shadowboxing and watching Uncle Chuck tactically hit a punching bag. Uncle Chuck won a welterweight title in his heyday, compared to a young Marvin Haggler for his speed and punching power. He buys David a pair of red boxing gloves and a punching bag for his ninth birthday. Uncle Chuck tells David to vent his frustrations on the punching bag when things bother him. He incidentally becomes street-smart by hanging out with Uncle

Chuck in the concrete jungle. He identifies con artists and shady people hustling throughout the New Haven projects.

The projects are a place where residents feel unsafe. Police presence is minimal. Uncle Chuck believes in protection. If the police cannot patrol the area, he figures citizens have the right to defend themselves. He purchases a thirty-eight special to safeguard himself from intruders. Stick-up kids in the projects will rob you and break into your home if given the opportunity, especially with limited policing. Chuck constantly reiterates if they break into his home, his two friends, Smith and Wesson, will politely introduce themselves. He seldom carries his gun with him.

On certain occasions, he will take David to a deserted field and let him watch as he fires holes through empty beer bottles he places in the area. David is fascinated as to how something so small can have so much impact, although Chuck never allows David to pull the trigger. He is too afraid he will accidentally shoot himself. Chuck keeps his gun in a secret location at all times. One summer afternoon, while Chuck walks to the corner store, David plays catch with his football in the kitchen, which is something Chuck is adamantly against. "Never play with the football in the kitchen," he constantly reminds David. David tosses the football in the air and runs forward to catch it. He has excellent hands and seldom drops anything. On his third toss-up, David reaches forward to grab the football and drops it. He bends down to where the football lands and notices the square tile flooring where the football has landed is a shade lighter than the rest of the brown tiles in the kitchen. David hits the football against the tile and hears a hollow

sound, which intrigues him. The square corners of the tile are misaligned. He removes the tile, finding a thick steel-plated covering underneath. After carefully removing the steel-plated cover, he discovers the silver thirty-eight special shining brightly before him. He then places everything back in its original position and never tells anyone. Uncle Chuck also gives him a crash course on sex at thirteen. He pays a different prostitute to lay with David every other Saturday, offering him a complete understanding of how to satisfy a woman. David learns the intricacies of prostitutes, their manipulation, and how persuasive they can be.

All in all, David reasons most women fit this description. The prostitutes teach him a valuable lesson. Love and sex exist as two different entities. Love has feelings, whereas sex has an unsatisfying urge to fulfill a want or desire. After countless escapades, he grows distrustful of women. He seeks love in women incapable of providing it, ultimately leaving him hollow.

The suburban experience is an eye-opener for David. Unlike the hood, white suburbia has garages bigger than Uncle Chuck's two-bedroom flat in the projects. Each neighbor looks out for the other. They value their property and won't hesitate to call the police if you don't belong. The nights are as quiet as the days. In the projects, most people sleep until midafternoon from hanging out all night, drinking, smoking, and selling drugs. David appreciates the quietness of suburbia, but he dislikes his Caucasian cousin Andrew. Andrew is a constant thorn in his side. David loves his aunt Rebecca. She makes David feel like part of the family. Aunt Rebecca resembles David's mother. She has Emerald green eyes. Her face is white as snow, with kinky red hair. David immediately clings to her, realizing she is the closest person to his mother. He's never had any problems with Aunt Rebecca. The problem derives from her son Andrew. Andrew has long red hair, freckles, and malicious bright blue eyes. Andrew spends the night at his grandmother's house on numerous occasions.

He calls David a "nigger" whenever his grandmother leaves the room. Andrew insists David doesn't belong in his family and wholeheartedly believes his blood isn't pure enough to be considered Caucasian. Andrew says his father hates black people, and his aunt died in a car accident because she was with a dumb nigger. David has built up animosity brewing more and more towards Andrew. He confides in his grandmother to do something soon. She dismisses the accusations against Andrew and tells David to stop listening to lies about Andrew from Uncle Chuck. David feels betrayed. His grandmother refuses to give him a fair chance to explain the situation but believes every lie Andrew tells her. David turns to Uncle Chuck for support. He advises David to pound Andrew's face if the word nigger comes out of his white trashy mouth again. David follows the instructions thoroughly. He breaks Andrew's nose, gives him a black eye, and punctures two ribs.

His grandmother finds Andrew bloodied and unresponsive on the living room rug. She passes out right next to Andrew. David screams for her to awaken, but she eventually dies from an acute stroke. He is extremely sorry for his actions. David apologizes and begs his family for forgiveness. The family turns against David. No one from his mother's family wants anything to do with him and ignores his plea. The family sends him off to a group home for troubled youth. *David has his reasons for not believing in God.*

CHAPTER 10

PAUL

Bedford Mental Institution

At this time, most of the visitors have cleared the room. I am once again left without a guest until the doctor approaches me. His cheap brute cologne smells awful. He's not the guest I'm looking for, but a guest nonetheless.

"Mr. Mitchell, are you ready for our session today?" *I'm not in a good mood today. My thoughts are with Alex and what she just shared with me. I'm ready to leave this place for good, but the perverted doctor stands in my path.*

"I'll follow you, doctor. Lead the way." *During our brief walk to his office, I wondered how he felt about Alex. My jealous side wants to ask him for his true intentions, although the other half doesn't like any part.*

The doctor's room is immaculate. A plush white carpet encircles the large office—sky blue drapes the walls, and beautiful watercolor paintings bring the room to life. I sit on a comfortable brown leather couch facing the opposite direction. I guess he doesn't find me as attractive as Alex. The strange-looking doctor sits behind me to start his question-and-answering session. His complexion is dark as the night, and he has a West Indies accent. He is tall with bulging brown eyes and a receding hairline. He looks to be in his mid-thirties. His skin is smooth but quite grotesque from a long scar on the right side of his face. The repugnant spot stretches several inches from his cheekbone, ending near his chin. His punctured flesh seems infected, as if it hasn't properly healed, and shaped like the letter c. The doctor's attire is formal. He's wearing a white tuxedo, which fits him perfectly, and a black bow tie. I imagine Alex facing him and squirming as she tries to withstand his unsightly scar while his eyes are agape, lusting for her.

"Mr. Mitchell, can you tell me again why you attempted to take your life?" *I have to clear the thought of him touching Alex. Let it go. I tell myself. Alex can handle herself just fine. I must focus on getting out of here, even if it means repeatedly telling my story. The same question I've answered a zillion times since my arrival. When will this end?*

"I've told you this already. You know the reason, doc." *Can you tell me why Alex is facing you in her sessions? That should be my question for you.*

"Mr. Mitchell, your situation is indeed a very serious one. Do I need to remind you your freedom relies on my approval of your condition? So, until I fully understand what led you to this point in your life, I will continue to ask it?" *He will continue to aggravate me. Every day that passes, she fades from my memory, and I don't need to talk about her. I only need to forget.*

"Do I have to start from the beginning?"

"Please, Mr. Mitchell, if you don't mind." *Oh, I mind, alright. Enough is enough.*

"I was introduced to Patricia Martin by one of the deacons at a church retreat. My church, including three other churches, decided to have a two-week revival. This revival occurred in a private wooded area on the outskirts of Woodbridge, Connecticut. The four churches provided food, shelter, and two weeks of praising God in a stress-free environment."

"What were your feelings upon meeting her for the first time?"

"I thought she was incredible. She has soft, dark brown eyes. Her wavy black hair was pulled back into a neat ponytail, revealing a round mocha cream face and two beautiful small dimples on each cheek. She wore a tangerine sheath dress along with black flats to match." *Five months have barely passed, and I can smell her scent. Why must he keep prying into my past?* "Patricia is very articulate. When I first heard her speak, I knew she had a solid educational background. She holds a master's degree in mass communications from Columbia University. Her thought-provoking conversation pulls me in right away. We talked about everything from politics to current events. Patricia firmly believes in affirmative action and says people equally qualified in the job market should be able to land decent jobs.

She further explained that women and minorities don't have a fair chance compared to whites. Rich white men run Wall Street and the corporate infrastructure. They choose to hire people similar to them, credentials or no credentials. The playing field must stay even, she demanded. She is a strong supporter of President Obama. Patricia stated President Obama has humanitarian characteristics, whereas Romney, his running mate, cares only about profit. She is also a Giant fan. We never missed a game on Sundays. I wore my number ten Eli Manning jersey, and she wore number eighty, Victor Cruz. When the Giants scored a touchdown, we cheered and hollered just like the fans on television."

"How did Patricia feel about you being a Pastor?"

"Patricia told me she seldom attends church because the minister's words don't move her. His sermons are more of theory, never relating the bible to real-life issues. When she did attend church, it was partly due to her feeling guilty. Patricia believes in God but is searching for a better experience. A close friend convinced her to come out and hear me preach. The experience lifts her spirit. My sermon sparked her heart, and she ultimately felt alive again. She claimed my words touched her. Patricia admired my decision to become a minister and said I preach very well. Patricia and I were two peas in a pod. She likes the things I like as well, and the things I don't like, she doesn't like them either. I thought she was truly an amazing person."

"So, I assume you connected quickly with her?" *Delight fills his voice. In a weirWeirdly, it turns him on to hear my misfortune.*

"Yes," I answer. *I want the doctor to stop, but the questions continue to roll off his tongue.* "Did you connect after the revival ended?"

"We connected like dots on a numbering coloring set. We went everywhere together. When we traveled, I made sure we slept in separate beds. I never touched her sexually. I respected Patricia and myself as Christians. Don't get me wrong. I'm only human. I yearned for her, but I wanted things to be right in God's eyes. I had to be near her constantly. And if she wasn't near me, I talked with her throughout the day. I was vulnerable, and she knew it."

"What changed, Mr. Mitchell?"

"When the honeymoon period ended, I began to see her true identity. She wanted more of me, but I couldn't give her more without marriage first. As a pastor, I told her it was impossible. She pressed me continually to make love to her and give her more than just my words. I am a man of faith, I told her. God has chosen me to impart his message on believers and unbelievers to help save them from sin."

"When you refused to give in, what did she do?" *No, the question is, what didn't she do? For one thing, sure, she made my life a living Hell.*

CHAPTER 11

The temperature in Hartford, Connecticut, is a frigid twenty-two degrees. Pedestrians scurry to their destinations, trying to outrun old man winter. A sheet of ice blankets the streets from

snowfall and rain the night before. Public Work trucks spray sand over treacherous roads to prevent accidents. The cold weather has not deterred China's faithful. China refuses to cancel the XL Center concert amid precautions from her doctor. The conversation is still fresh in her memory. "MS can flare up at a moment's notice. You can be onstage performing and suddenly have a severe episode. The protective layers around your nerve fibers are slowly deteriorating. When this fully disrupts your nerves, you can lose function in any body part."

"What about my voice? My voice is my survival."

"I think your voice will be okay, but I'm more concerned about your coordination. You can lose the ability to walk."

"Well, I feel fine so far."

"I think you should rest more until I run additional tests. That way, we can get you the proper medication and therapy."

"I have fans. They need me, and I need them."
"I understand China. You do what you must, but I'm strongly against it."

"I feel wonderful. I've rested for two full days. I'm ready for the road. My fans await me," the female Indian doctor doesn't press the issue any further.

China detests doctors. Doctors make things much worse than they appear to be. China is in the best shape of her life. She looks out of the luxury Hilton Hotel window to view the sights of downtown Hartford. Unlike New York, Texas, and California, the nightlife is busy for a small state. Connecticut has a lot to offer its residents. The center of Hartford has many restaurants and clubs on every corner to accommodate your stomach and somewhere to burn it off afterward. A knock on the door brings her back to reality.

"Who is it?"

"Kelly," China lets her in. Kelly is wearing a black jumpsuit with black heels. Her straight blond wig touches her shoulders, bringing out her dark & lovely complexion. Kelly's brown eyes do a thorough examination of China. She checks her up and down for any signs of exhaustion.

"How do you feel China?" Her question is serious.
"I feel great. The two days of rest did wonders for me."
"You don't have to do this, you know," China smiles at Kelly reassuringly.

"I'm China Reynolds, one of the greatest vocalists around. I have sold twenty million units worldwide. I have endorsement deals from Maybelline, Victoria's Secret, and Infiniti. My name packs arenas. So many loyal fans love me. I've made up my mind."

Kelly remembers the first time she heard China sing, the innocent little girl with an overpowering voice. She gained control of the audience as soon as her mouth opened. Back then, Kelly was just twenty-five years of age. She tagged along with her music producer father, learning everything possible when pinpointing talented artists. He explained to her what to look for in a singer. They must have stage presence, vocal pitch, and the ability to move an audience. Kelly discovered China by coincidence one morning while attending church. She considers herself a part-time Christian.

She makes a conscious effort to attend church on the first of each month and Easter Sunday. New members are joining the church throughout the year. Kelly knows a handful of members, but not everyone. The church has four choirs: the young adult choir, men's choir, mass choir, and children's choir. The children's choir has to perform on a warm Easter.

Sunday in April. Sharply dressed are 500 people in attendance. New Easter outfits circulate throughout the pews.

A few members need to cut the tags hanging from their new threads, allowing snooping members in the congregation to know the price. Handheld fans are waving like butterfly wings because of the hot temperature inside. The heavy-set black female choir director, wearing a white robe and a crinkled blue-collar shirt, signals the children to stand. Five girls and five boys in blue shirts and white pants arise. Without warning, China begins singing "Amazing Grace" to the congregation's delight. Her powerful voice reverberates inside the church, receiving immediate attention. She reaches notes seasoned singers would envy. Women yell hallelujah, wiping their eyes with a tissue, and some even drop to their knees, calling out to Jesus. All five hundred stand in the aisles listening to an angel. Kelly has never heard a child sing in this fashion. China's singing sprouts Goosebumps over Kelly's body. When the song ends, a standing ovation lasts nearly five minutes. The congregation wants more of her. Kelly follows China to the parking lot after the service. A short-haired woman, sporting a silver chain linked to a silver cross and carrying a black King James Bible, cuts her off before reaching China.

"May I help you with something? Henrietta asks rudely, turning up her lips. "How long has she been singing?"

"I didn't get your name, mam," Henrietta interjects.

"Oh, I apologize. I'm Kelly Anderson," she offered her handshake. Henrietta glares at her hand disgustingly and turns her head. Kelly feels awkward but continues her pitch.

"I'm a music producer. I'm looking for the next big star."

"Not interested," Henrietta says, hurrying away and grabbing China by the hand.

"Are you her grandmother?" Kelly blurts out, presuming she appears too old to be her mother. Henrietta grudgingly stops in her tracks, spinning around on her heels.

"I'm her legal guardian, her mother. We are not interested in what you have to offer. My child has a gift from the lord. She sings for God, not for Satan."

"Can you just hear me out?" Kelly pleads.

"What for? I've heard it all before. Others like you have tried to convince me, but I'm no fool. We don't need your money or your lies. Good day, mam. God bless you!" She quickly directs China near the car. China takes a hurried glimpse at Kelly when Henrietta walks around the vehicle. Kelly detects the masked pain in China's eyes in search of freedom of expression. Her mother holds her captive, a "Holy Roly" with tons of attitude dictating her child's future, conversely stifling China's growth. Kelly recognizes the signs. The converted sanctified Christian. After living in countless sins, she has the nerve to judge everyone else?

Her tactics don't scare Kelly. She has seen it all too often in men and women who shelter their children from the real world—five years passed before Kelly saw China again. China presents herself at Kelly's doorstep in rags. Her hair is messy, her clothes stained from wearing them numerous days a row, and her face is unclean. She ran away from home. Henrietta prevents her from singing altogether. Her mother wants her to forget about singing and concentrate more on serving God. Henrietta's twisted logic insists the devil seized China's gift of voice. He is using her voice to gain more souls for his kingdom.

"I want to sing and be a star like the singers on the radio," she says, desperately standing in Kelly's doorway. The small, innocent girl with hazel eyes has matured into a beautiful teen.

"Are you sure, China?" Kelly asks, watching her fidget with her hands.

"I'm positive. Singing is all I ever wanted in life."

"Why did you come to me instead of going to someone else after all this time?" China hunches up her shoulders.

"I don't know. I guess you look trustworthy. Your face doesn't lie when you talk." "Lie when I talk?"

"Yes, like the others before you. When they say things about singing, their eyes wander off a lot. I don't believe them. I believe you, though."

"What about mom?"

"I'm thirteen now. I'm grown. I can do whatever I please. I love my mom. She's just hard to live with. I'll keep in touch with her. Can we start making music right now?" Her eyes sparkle.

"You're grown? You might sound like an adult, but you're far from it. I can get in big trouble by having you here. I think we should call Mom."

"If you call her, I will run away again. I'll never stay with her. I want to be a star. Why can't you make me a star?" She begs.

"China, your mother can say I kidnapped you."

"Well, if she does, you can say she abuses me."

"I will not tell that type of lie, young lady. It's dishonest."

"If you send me back to her, you will miss out on making tons of money." "I have money, China. Maybe not tons of it, but I'm doing quite alright."

"If you would just sign me to a recording contract, I promise you I will contact my mother in time," Kelly studies her.

"I tell you what; if you go back home and attend school regularly, I will start recording you. It's the only option I can offer. Take it or leave it."

"I guess I have to take it. I want to be famous."

"First, we have to get you out of those clothes. Secondly, you can use a bath. Thirdly, I have to make sure you haven't lost your voice. It happens to the best singers," China stares at her in bewilderment.

"I sing better than the last time you saw me."

"Prove it, young lady," Kelly insists."

"What would you like to hear?" China asks coyly.

"Amazing grace."

"I have to warn you."

"Warn me about what?"

"I'm not responsible if you collapse from feeling the Holy Ghost," China laughs.

"Whatever, girl, sing the song," Kelly grins. *China gently clears her throat, letting out her gift from God. Kelly's Goosebumps are much bigger than before. Her heart catches fire. She is listening to the voice of an angel. Kelly gazes at China inside the luxurious Hilton hotel room. China's bold arrogance has taken over her once-youthful innocence.*

CHAPTER 12

DAVID

Cedric and David have just finished working out inside the weight room facility. They are sitting in the lounge area discussing tonight's game against Toronto.

"Dave, our opponent has a great defensive front. You'll have to work hard to gain yards." "We have to mix things up a bit. A little pass and a little run to keep them off balance."

"I think that'll work," Cedric smiles approvingly. "By the way, how's everything going with Cathy?"

"I'd rather not talk about it," he says, disappointed. Cedric couldn't believe what he was hearing. "I thought you told me she was the one for you? You said…"

"I know what I said," David interjects. He tilts his head back in the seat, staring at the ceiling.

"Hey, easy, David. Don't take my head off."

"Pay me no mind. I'm a little stressed," David rubs his hands over his face. "Stressed over Cathy? I would enjoy that type of stress. She is something special, dude." "I can't deny that she isn't, but it's deeper than that," he shakes his head.

"Is she pregnant? I know how you feel about the kid thing. You told me you're not ready to start a family yet," he asks, raising his thick eyebrows.

"No, it's not that."

"Does she have another man on the side?"
"No way, she's loyal."

"Yeah, that's what they all say. Remember when Katrina played me for my brother? She was supposed to be loyal, too. The problem is she loves sex. It doesn't matter where she gets it from as long as she gets it. I was too in love at the time to notice."

"Cedric, she would never cheat."

"You don't know that."

"I certainly do."

"How, so?"

"For one thing, you have to have sex to cheat," Cedric drops his thick bottom lip. "You're not having sex, David?"

"No."

"Now, I understand. I don't blame you for being upset. I would be upset, too. How long have you been without sex?"

"A little over a month."
"After a few more weeks, if she doesn't let you inside, let her ass go."
"Cedric, please stop. I like her a lot. It's not the sex."
"Then why are you so upset?"
"Religion."
"A church sister? Hell no!"
"Hell, yes!"

"A church sister is the worst. They always preach and criticize everyone else while their lives are upside down. There are a bunch of hypocrites if you ask me. Constantly quoting scripture and never living by it. They use Bible passages to fit their own needs."

"How do you know so much about it?"
"I dated this girl once from church. Let me tell you what she did."
"Another one?"
"Her name was Shirley Skeezer."
"Are you referring to Shirley Caesar, the gospel singer?"

"Nah, her real name is Shirley Jackson. I gave her the name Shirley Skeezer because of the cheating thing. She told me she was a straight-up virgin serving God until I caught her on her knees between the legs of some brother in the church. She gave a new meaning of speaking in tongues."

"You crazy as hell," David laughs out loud.
"What did Cathy say?" His laughter stops.
"She wants me to go to church with her."

"What's wrong with that? I would go anywhere with Cathy. I'm sure you've been to church before. How hard can it be?"

"No.
"Never?"
"Never."
"You believe in God, right?"
"No."
"Wow, a football-playing atheist? You've got to be kidding me, right?"
"I kid you not."
"Why?"
"I have my reasons. Just leave it at that."

"Well, I'm no one to judge, too each his own. What will you do?"

"I broke it off."

"What? Are you crazy? You know how good that woman looks?"

"Yeah, I do."

"Wow, I don't know what to say, David. I'll just leave it alone. By the way, what time are we meeting at the field tonight?"

"8:00."

"I'll be there."

"OK, see you later."

CHAPTER 13

PAUL
Bedford Mental Institution

"One chilly night in December, Patricia invited me to discuss our situation. Before meeting with her, I spoke to her over the phone. She said she respected my faith, understood God comes first before all things, and that marriage would be the right thing to do before consummating our relationship. Upon hearing this, my feelings grew even stronger. I realized she was the one for me."

"So what happened next, Mr. Mitchell?"

"When I knocked on the front door of her condominium, the door inched open. I called out her name, not wanting to go in unannounced. After calling her name at least six to seven times with no answer, I wasn't sure what to do. I don't like surprises. I've seen too many scenes similar to this one in movies. The actor or actress has no idea what awaits them behind the door. I'd never been in her home before. We usually meet at my place, or if I had to pick her up, I waited for her in the car. After mustering up enough confidence, I finally decided to go in."

"What happened after you went inside?"

"The smell of potpourri and cinnamon hit my nostrils once inside. I hear soft music from Luther Vandross playing "A House is Not a Home," so I walk down the narrow corridor following the music trail. Patricia's house is impeccable, and everything is in order. The music led me to her bedroom. Her bedroom door is exposed. She lay naked on silk sheets, stroking her curves and caressing her breasts. She calls out my name. Patrica surprised me with her nakedness and the perfect contours of her lovely body. Patricia begged me to lie down with her. I had triumphed over my desires with years of celibacy, praying that God would send me the right woman. My longing for her made it impossible for me to stop. I did everything she asked of me. We made love for hours, intertwined like two people sharing the same breath. Patricia is a passionate lover. She led, and I followed. She did things to me I never experienced before. It was the last time I saw Patricia Martin."

"How did this make you feel, Paul?"

"It damaged me for a while. I opened my heart to Patricia and let her into my world. She dismissed me like I didn't matter. She caused a lot of pain for me. Subsequently, I stayed to myself, concentrating more on saving souls."

"Did you ever hear from her again?"

"No, I called her many times, leaving messages on her voicemail. I even wrote a long letter stating how much I missed her. She didn't return my calls or respond to my letter. I then decided to go by her home. I knocked on her door, and a Hispanic man opened the door. I asked for Patricia, and he told me he didn't know anyone by that name. He said he'd just moved in last month. I was devastated. I then poured myself into my work, gaining more followers as the church congregation increased." *It's difficult for me to continue. Panic clutches me. I struggle to get my words out.* "Maybe...two months had passed since I'd last seen her...before that unforgettable morning."

"Please explain."

I can't talk about it anymore. The pain and confusion is coming back to me. My head is spiraling in circles. I hear my heart hammering through my chest. Sweat dampens my brow. The sudden change in my voice alarms the doctor.

"Paul, are you ok?"

"I just need a little water. I'll be fine."

"Have you taken your meds today?"

"I don't believe in pills. God will take care of me."

"God has taken care of you by allowing his plants to have the proper ingredients used in medicine to help calm you. The recent traumatic events you've experienced have given you a certain amount of anxiety. The pills will help offset this. If you want to, Paul, you can take the meds as a parachute only when your panic attacks flare up. Would that make you feel better about taking the pill?"

"Not exactly, but what choice do I have to stop this uneasiness inside me?" *My body is shaking like a leaf, and I can't control it.*

"Give me a few minutes, Paul. I will call the nurse to bring the pills.

Do I need drugs? I've never had an illness like this before. Am I that far gone to succumb to this condition? I am a man of faith, and nothing is impossible with God. So why am I contemplating taking pills? Maybe the doctor's right. Plants were put here by God to help us. The thin brunette nurse arrives quickly. She smiles, batting her blue eyes, then hands me a glass of water and one Xanax pill to swallow. I place the pill on my tongue, watching the nurse as if waiting for her approval. I hold the glass of water up to my mouth. I then close my eyes, taking a sip while letting the pill reach my stomach. The nurse tells me the medication will take twenty minutes before it starts kicking in. I'm not sure if I can hold out for twenty minutes.

CHAPTER 14

CHINA

XL Center Hartford, Connecticut

China sashays around the stage, interacting with her faithful. Her female dancers wear black with silver boots and silver hats to match. China's short silver mini skirt and low-cut black top reveal enough eye candy, triggering the excited males in the front row to salivate. The eight female dancers clap their hands, rallying the crowd as China's female ensemble delivers a lively tune.

"Hartford, are you ready!" China shouts to the audience through the microphone. The sixteen thousand plus fans scream a resounding "Yeah." China motions the band to lower the music. "I'm sorry for my absence. Tonight, I will make it up to you. You have supported me throughout my entire career, and it is very much appreciated. Without you, I am nothing," she presses her hand against her heart to say thanks. Her eyes moisten. "My fans come first. Everything else is second. Let's get this party started!"

The band plays the instrumental from "Come Love Me," China's number-one hit. Eager fans rush to the front of the stage, getting a better view of the sexy diva. The ones remaining in their seats are standing and swaying from side to side. "Come Love Me" is an up-tempo song China wrote during a distressing breakup with her ex-boyfriend of five years. Mark Chambers wants to marry China and have children. China doesn't feel the timing is right. Her music career is soaring. Marriage and children will slow her success. Her fans deserve more of her time. Mark

can wait; at least, that's what she assumed. The breakup occurs backstage at one of her previous shows.

"I can't do this anymore, China. How long do I have to wait?"

"Mark, please give me a little more time. I have a new music out. I have to tour. My fans need me, and I need them."

"It's always about your fans. Does anything matter besides your fans? Do I matter? Does your mother matter? How about your friends? We don't matter, right? You put everyone last. God forbid if something happens where you can't perform. I wonder what will happen to your fans then."

"Mark, please understand. My fans put money in my pocket. They pay my bills. Without them, I'm nothing. My fans were there when my dad left and when my mother refused to let me sing. I owe them the world", she stresses her point.

"You don't owe them anything. All it takes is a bad CD; your fans will forget you existed. Admirers follow who's hot at the moment. When you turn cold, you'll see for yourself!"

"How can you say that to me? Turn cold? I'll never turn cold! I see now, Mark. You want me to fail so you can have me all for yourself. You're a selfish individual, you know that?"

"I'm selfish? I haven't seen you for weeks, and you have the nerve to call me selfish? I'm selfish for wanting to marry you and start a family. Where are your priorities? You know what, China?"

"What, Mark?"
"I had about enough of this. Marry your fans. I'm not important to you."
"Mark, please give me more time. I love you."

"The only thing you love is your fans; you've proved it. Your time is up." China regrets not giving in to Mark, as she misses him daily. She gets the crowd's attention.

"Ladies, move your hands from side to side if a man has broken your heart, if a man has done you wrong if a man has cheated on you, or if a man has flat out left you," thousands of women move their hands from side to side in harmony.

"This song is about someone that hurt me. He broke my heart, and he left me. If you can feel my pains, then sing along with me. *"Come love me the way I want to be loved, come love me with more than kisses and hugs, come love me unlike you've never loved before, come love me and give me more and more. Respect my life and the things accompanying it; if you love this, you'll wait to get it. My singing profession is how I survive; if you can't understand, it is time to try. Come love me..."*

China points her microphone toward the sea of voices inside the arena. She listens to a perfect-sounding blend of sopranos and altos, combining in a flawless accord. She glances over the sea of faces, thinking about Mark. He will come back to her as he always did after they argued. Mark is easygoing and a kind-hearted person. He always stays away for a week. Tonight makes two weeks, and China feels a twinge of nervousness in the pit of her stomach. She met Mark during a radio station contest. The eighteenth caller had to call hot ninety-two point one in Buckland, Pennsylvania County, in the allotted time to win a backstage pass and a night out with China. Incidentally, Mark had called the radio station to request a favorite song, unaware of the contest. To his surprise, the DJ announced he'd just won a backstage pass to meet China Reynolds. Mark listens to music in his downtime.

Sitting in his single-family home, he finds it relaxing, taking in the sultry sounds of Neo Soul Music. He's seen China in videos and heard many of her latest hits. Mark doesn't consider himself an enthusiast. It baffles him when fans become obsessed over a songstress. From stalking them to dressing in the same apparel, Mark had never been one of these persons. He considers performers to be just as human as the next person. Superstars eat, dress, sleep, and clean themselves like the rest of society. The night out with China is something he will never forget as long as he lives.

The rules are straightforward. It states the winner will accompany China to a restaurant of her choosing, paid for by the station. China modifies the rules according to her liking. She persuades the limo driver to find a secluded club. She needs to remain low-key and avoid violence and TMZ. The young Vietnamese limo driver named Lee, who doesn't look a day over twenty, smiles through the rearview mirror, nodding his head and obeying her command like a rookie in training. He implies he knows a great spot where she won't have any problems. She passes a hundred-dollar bill up front, thanking him. China's small arsenal of bodyguards follows behind closely, driving black-tinted BMW trucks.

"Wouldn't you prefer to go dancing than to eat dinner?" She excitedly asks Mark.

"It doesn't matter to me," Mark anxiously says, noticing her appealing features. He has seen her pictures in magazines and countless television appearances, which portray only glimpses of her attractiveness. In-person, he thinks she is much more beautiful.

"Oh, I almost forgot. You won the ticket, not me. So if you want to go to a restaurant, it's fine with me, your choice. I just want to have a good time and be comfortable," Mark is undoubtedly having a good time and somewhat uncomfortable. It isn't every day he has a woman of this magnitude sitting next to him in a Hummer limousine. Mark had a few girlfriends over the

years, but they weren't even close compared to China. China has an effervescent personality and Sensual eyes. The women Mark dated in the past were stiff, and their looks were lifeless, along with their character. China exudes confidence. He's delighted to be around her.

"I'm just a country boy deep down inside. The city life is sort of foreign to me. Lavish restaurants, fancy clubs, and big bright lights were never my thing growing up. I'm more of a homebody. If you want to take me dancing, it's alright."

"Well, country boy, I'm going to give you a dance lesson you will never forget," she smiles, studying him from head to toe.

"By the way, country boy, what's your name?" She asks, gently biting her bottom lip. "It's Mark Chambers."

"Nice to meet you, Mark Chambers, I'm China Reynolds," she grins. "So Mark, what do you do for a living?"

"I'm a fireman."

"Will you be able to put my fire out tonight?" She teases. Mark is unsure of what to say. Her question catches him off guard. She notices his awkwardness.

"You don't have to answer that. Sometimes I get carried away. I think what you do for a living is magnificent. You put your life on the line to save others. I admire you for that. Have you ever had any close calls while trying to rescue someone?"

"I've had one close call. Two children remained trapped inside a burning kitchen." "Wow, if it were me, I would've lost it. How did the fire start?"

"The fire started when the eldest sibling tried to cook French fries while mom was out grocery shopping. The gas burner was up too high, so it caused the pan to spill over grease, which contacted the gas burner, igniting paper plates left on the stove." The thought of being rescued by this handsome man sends chills through her body. She feels warm and tingly inside. He smells so good to her. "The boys tried to put the grease fire out using clothing to fan it. The fire spread quickly, and the children panicked."

"Poor children, they must have been horrified. The thought of dying there all alone and no one to save them. How could a mom leave her children by themselves? Someone should punish her to the fullest degree possible. I hate parents who neglect their children! It's just not right. Do you know what I mean?" Her display of pain is prominent, and it consumes her appearance.

"I certainly do," he looks at her strangely. Her wounds remain open, and he wonders if her anguish stems from firsthand experience. He ponders if she suffered the same fate as a child. China detects him examining her and abruptly straightens up.

"When we arrived, the flames were escaping through every window. The house was beginning to fall apart. We didn't have much time before the roof collapsed. The children were screaming for help. We quickly cut down the door to dispel some of the heat and smoke. I ran inside, searching for the children as their cries for help grew louder. I followed their voices. I found them pinned in the kitchen corner from the stove. Heavy flames surrounded their boundary, leaving them no escape." His pronunciation is soothing as China holds onto every syllable. She can listen endlessly to the sound of his voice. She trails the movement of his thin lips, craving for a kiss.

"The fire hose made the boundary safe enough to reach the children. I ran into the kitchen corner with blankets to wrap around the children before attempting our escape. I carried the

eldest child, and my partner carried the youngest. We made it outside safely without any injuries right before the roof collapsed."

"You were lucky. It could've been much worse."

"I don't believe luck had anything to do with it. I believe God provided our escape." "I think you're right, country boy," she nods.

"I know I'm right. If it wasn't for God, where would I be?" He replies, self-assured. "That's true...where would we all be?" The trajectory of her voice diminishes.

"You didn't say that with a lot of confidence." China doesn't like where the conversation is heading. The thought of her mother carrying her bible and preaching everywhere she traveled disrupted her good mood. Soon, he will be asking her about the church. She has to change the subject fast.

"God has given me the ability to sing and dance. Without him, I wouldn't be who I am today," China hopes what she just said satisfies him.

"I think God leads us into the path we should take, but many of us miss the turn. We can see the turn up ahead, and then we decide to take a shortcut and search for a faster way to succeed and fail miserably. Once failure sets in, our attempts to reroute become difficult," he sounds like a pastor to China and nothing like a fireman. China needs the limo driver to hurry. She encourages him.

"Lee, how much longer?"

"Three minutes, it's around the corner, Ms. Reynolds." *Just in time, young man. Just in time. China says to herself.*

"Lee, that was fast. If you get us back just as fast, I have another crisp C-note waiting for you."

"I will do my best, Ms. Reynolds," he cracks a big smile in the rearview mirror. China doesn't miss her opportunity to alter the subject.

"So, Mark, do you have happy or sad feet?"

"In between feet, it depends on the song." Mark is an average dancer. It takes a while for him to get going. He adds more variety to his comfortable two-step move if the right song is playing. Born in the country, he spent most of his teenage years tending to his parent's farm. Mark enjoys country living and the rugged terrain of Pennsylvania farmland. He appreciates working with his hands, his definition of a real man. Mark tills the land, feeds the animals, and stores the milk and eggs ready to be sold. Even as a teen, he shied away from the quickened pace of the city. While his friends were partying every other night, Mark concentrated on his studies and his commitment to his parent's farm. Mark preferred to stay home and read. His favorite books to read were fitness magazines. Mark spent his weekly allowance on bodybuilding books. The walls inside his room contain pictures of bodybuilders. Mark is a fitness fanatic. At the age of eighteen, he was able to bench press three hundred pounds. Mark looks intimidating to most men. Though, underneath the hulking exterior lives a gentle giant. He didn't have much social life back then, but it never bothered him. Family is more important.

"What special song will it take to get your feet in motion, country boy?"

"I'm not a huge rap fan, but I enjoy some rap music. I like to listen to Drake, Rick Ross, and Jay-Z. If one of their songs plays tonight, my feet will respond accordingly," he chuckles.

"You don't strike me as someone into rap music. You have a sophisticated appeal and look more like someone into Maxwell, Music Soul Child, and Sade," she says, checking out his smooth almond complexion.

"I'm really into Neo-Soul music, but when I want to dance, I need something catchy to move to. I can wear tight skinny jeans sagging to my knees, showing my draws, and sport some gold fronts if you want?" Mark is beginning to warm up to China.

"No, thank you, country boy. One little Wayne is enough," Mark laughs at the idea. "Are you sure, China?" He clowns.

"Positive," she gives him a disturbing look. China is having fun, and so is he.

"I'll make sure the DJ plays one of your songs. Don't be shy tonight, country boy," she teases. The limo driver pulls up behind an abandoned warehouse. He quickly gets out and knocks on a rusted black door. The door squeaks open as he goes inside. In less than five minutes, he reappears, opening the limo door. He grins feverishly at China.

"Is it safe to go in, Lee?"

"It's one of the safest clubs in Pennsylvania. I know the owner. I told him you were coming in. He freaked out."

"I don't have to worry when I get inside, do I?" China feels edgy.
"Not at all. It's a nice atmosphere and your type of crowd."
"OK, Lee, I trust your words. Show us the way."

Her bodyguards go in first to make sure the abandoned warehouse is safe. Two White male guards cover the front door, and two black male guards cover the rear. The remaining three
guards are outside, awaiting the signal to come in. The guards stay as close to China and Mark as possible. Dressed in black clothing comparable to army fatigues, each guard has an earpiece to stay in contact with each other if something goes wrong. Once inside, China and Mark must take an elevator eight flights down. When they step off the elevator, the warehouse is alive and well. Outside of the warehouse, not a single car or person is in sight. China and Mark later discover reservations are for affluent individuals. It's a secret high society. The club and parking garage, hidden underground, keep the expensive vehicles concealed. China snatches Mark's hand and walks through the crowded dance area. She allows her guards to clear some needed space. Her bodyguards block half of the dance floor. The crowd doesn't seem to mind as long as they can get a glimpse of her. Once the partygoers realize what is occurring, they stop dancing and pull their phones out

to take pictures. Mark is getting a first-hand look at what it feels like to be a celebrity. He watches men and women push their way for an open space to get near China. Her bodyguards are well aware of the mayhem and keep a close watch.

Within minutes, two oversized white women dressed in spandex push through the mob, knocking down a few people. A few fallen petite victims think twice about retaliating, cursing under their breath. The two female bruisers appear to be sisters, both wearing pink lipstick and light blue eye shadow. Bruiser number one has long black hair, and bruiser number two has short blond hair. Standing as close as the guards permit, the sisters mimic China's moves. Mark becomes irritated from so many cell phones flashing.

"Do you want everyone taking pictures? Don't worry about someone putting your picture all over social media?" He yells over the music. Flirting with Mark, she bats her eyes and starts dancing seductively. China positions both hands on her curvy hips and gives Mark a long, lustrous stare before getting close enough to respond in his ear.

"Mark, it's all about pleasing my fans. I don't mind one bit, handsome," Mark is nervous. He thinks of pinching himself to make sure he isn't dreaming. China Reynolds is flirting with him and teaching him how to dance.

"Loosen up, big guy, and let the music take control," China surveys Mark's body. She can't believe how buffed he is.

"You have rhythm. You just need to be more in tune with the sound. Let your emotions take over."

"Ok, I'll try," Mark attempts to dance with more emotion, but he fails to impress China. "Watch and learn, country boy."

"China's moves are something exceptional to watch. She moves like a beautiful, faultless ballerina. She blazes the dance floor, doing steps Mark could never achieve with years of practice. The two sisters weep tears of joy. Mark stands back, giving China the floor to do her dance routine. After Mark's first memorable date, there were many more to follow. China enjoys his company. He makes her feel normal and brings her back to earth. He doesn't view China as a megastar but sees an imperfect woman learning from her mistakes as she goes along. Her larger-than-life persona does not affect him. He has grown to love her. And in turn, she has done the same. It is difficult for him to believe China is single. She has no one, but Mark is untrusting of her bodyguard.

"China, can I ask you a personal question?"

"What if I say no?" She teases.

"Then I'll have to respect your answer and keep it to myself."

"Will your question upset me?"

"I don't know, but it's kind of important."

"Is it important to you or important to me?"

"I think it's important to both of us if we continue in this relationship." "It's that important?"

"Yes."

"Ok, ask it then."

"Have you ever had a relationship with Jason?" He asks with a stone face.

"Look at you; you're jealous of Jason. I can't believe it. That's a first. I've never had anyone ask me that before," she giggles.

"I'm serious, China, have you?" He glares at her.

"I've never had a relationship with Jason, honey. There's nothing to worry about. I'm all yours. You can relax, Mark."

"Are you telling me the truth? The way Jason grills me makes me feel uncomfortable."

"Mark, I'm telling you the truth. Jason is only doing his job, honey, and he does it very well. He keeps the weird people and psychopaths away from me. Jason is my top bodyguard. I don't travel anywhere without him," the strain on Mark's face loosens a bit.

"I'm not overly jealous; you're a superstar, and I get it. Who am I to tell you who you can and cannot be around? I'm just an average Joe. I'm not even in your league. When you chose to be with me, I couldn't believe it. Sometimes, I still can't believe it. I'm very flattered, but Jason makes me edgy. He asks like he's a jealous ex-boyfriend. I don't like him around us when we're together. He watches me the entire time and never takes his eyes off me."

"You have to understand. We live in a crazy society, and people are constantly committing crimes daily. Celebrities have money, and I have money, the more reason for tight security."

"I understand that China, but Jason knows who I am. He knows that you and I are together. He tries to intimidate me, and I don't appreciate it," China cracks a weak smile.

"He's not trying to intimidate you. Jason likes you a lot. He talks about you when you're not around, all good things."

"Yeah, I bet." Mark turns his lips to the side. So what does he say about me?" She rubs her hand across Mark's massive bicep.

"He said a fan would be foolish to try anything with you around. He admires your physique. He thinks your body looks like the Rock."

"Honestly, is that all he says?"

"Yes, Mark, that's it. He's very fond of you. He said we make a great couple." "That's hard for me to believe."

"Well, believe it, honey. Can we not talk about this anymore?"

"Ok, but just tell him to ease up a bit."

"I will. I promise."

On his days off, China made it her obligation to get Mark a private box seat to watch her performances. Her jet would fly Mark to any tour date location. He wasn't exactly thrilled about airplanes, but China had a way of convincing him. After that, he became a frequent flyer. Back inside the sold-out arena, Mark hears the cheers from his XL center box seat. Two weeks have passed, and not a word from him.

He refuses to be second to her fans. Mark trusts his decision.

He came to see her perform one last time. It's setting in that she doesn't need him. China has money, luxury, and all the amenities fame and fortune have to offer. He can never give her any of these things. He is an average working-class citizen and makes decent money as a fireman, but not the money China Reynolds is used to. The tabloids wrote stories of how he would take her for every cent and reported he was living off her riches. The slanderous reports infuriated Mark. He supports himself and doesn't rely on anyone. Deep down inside, he understands China is on an entirely different level. Celebrity belongs with celebrity. The rich should be with the rich. He cannot offer her anything but his love, which seems pricey enough. An uncanny feeling arises in Mark as he makes his way to the door.

He feels betrayed, a total loss of five years in a relationship China snubbed from growing into something meaningful. He opens the box seat door to leave, then stops to listen to her voice one last time. There is silence in the arena. The raucous noise from her fans has died out. He strolls toward the box office window. His conscience tells him not to look and to let her go. She is happier with her fans. Mark presumes he's temporary, and her fans are long-term. He scans the XL Center Arena and witnesses the jubilation drained from her fans. Her fans look as if they've seen a ghost. Emergency personnel and her bodyguards hover around China, lying in the center of the stage. Mark wants to be on stage, holding her hand and giving her words of encouragement. Mark offered support when she lost the feeling in her legs a few shows prior. He carried China off stage amid the name-calling and displeasure from the audience. Mark has known about her condition for some time. She hid her illness from him. The doctor explained to Mark that China had a 50-50 chance of losing her ability to walk. He waited for China to confide in him, but she never did. Mark is confident her career is over. Her loyal fans will betray her. Mark opens the door and exits the room, never turning back.

"MS. Reynolds, can you stand?" The young black female paramedic asks.

"No, I can't feel my legs. Please carry me off the stage. I don't want my fans to see me like this."

"Ok, we will put you on a gurney."

"Carry me, please. I don't want a gurney. Where is Mark? Somebody get Mark!" She screams.

"Mark isn't here," Jason responds.

"Jason, please pick me up, I demand. Get me out of here."

"I have to follow protocol, MS. Reynolds. The gurney is for your safety." "Mark, Mark!" She shrieks. "Where are you?"

CHAPTER 15

DAVID

The locker room chant echoes from the football team. David rapidly leads the chant "Win or go home" among his fired-up teammates before the big game. David remembers his first time running with a football tucked underneath his arm. It was a youth midget football practice. Uncle Chuck volunteered that year as a football coach. He loved to coach children in any sport, but football and boxing were his passions. They both required a great deal of physicality, which he loved. Uncle Chuck learned the game of football from watching Monday night football and playing the sport on dirt fields in projects that feel identical to concrete. The parents appreciate his stern voice in addition to his rigid coaching style. He transformed timid children into strong, fierce gladiators on the football field. Some children cried initially but eventually became accustomed to his coaching style. When it was all said and done, he developed as their role model on and off the field. During that time, David was smaller than most of the children who participated. His growth spurt hadn't begun yet. Uncle Chuck thinks David is physically inept to be playing football.

His bones are growing but not to the point of taking hits by bigger children. At first, David's grandmother strongly disapproved of David going with Uncle Chuck, but she gave in when Chuck promised he wouldn't let David play. David accompanies Uncle Chuck to every practice. He carries the extra footballs and makes sure each player has a sufficient amount of water. He studies the methods critically and pays close attention to everything Uncle Chuck teaches on the football field.

"Uncle Chuck, when can I play?" David whines.

"Little man, you're not big enough yet. And one more thing, if you get hurt, your grandmother will have my head on a silver platter."

"I'm a big boy, Uncle Chuck. I'm solid. I can do twenty pushups every day," Chuck can see the courage in David's eyes. He hates disappointing him but can't risk losing David in court. If he is injured, his visitation rights will undoubtedly end.

"You keep doing those pushups, David, and one day you'll be stronger than me, alright?" "Does that mean I can play?"

"You can play when you grow a little more. It takes time and hard work."

David sees right through his Uncle. He is a lousy liar. David understands his uncle has no intention of ever letting him play football. His grandmother's words etched in stone keep him off the gridiron, and he can do nothing to change it. David's fate changes one afternoon in late August. While Chuck's practice is in session, the younger children who were not allowed to play gather together on a rundown field behind the practice field to play their own game of football. A few parents are there to make sure the children are safe. On this occasion, David decides to sneak away from the practice field and play with the other children, looking closely for Uncle Chuck. This particular afternoon, there are more parents around than usual. The parents are watching their little ones compete while cheering on their up-and-coming stars.

It tickles each parent how funny their little ones look trying to run with a football as big as they are until David runs with the ball. David sprints like a child possessed. His little body moves with great precision and accuracy. He makes cutbacks, hurdling over a few children in his path. Each time he runs with the ball, he is untouched. The parents in the bleachers can only watch in awe. David's prowess on the field reaches his uncle very quickly. Chuck's practice has just ended. He is packing his equipment bag when a parent approaches.

"Hey Chuck, can I holler at you for a moment?" Chuck prefers little conversation after his practice. The temperature and constant teaching usually have him drained. Talking is the furthest thing on his mind. His mind thinks of nothing but a cold beer and a cool shower. Parents are never satisfied. If Chuck accepts his conversation, he will have to listen to him rant about his grandson's lack of playing time, how his grandson is picked on by the other children, or better yet, why he doesn't allow his grandson to play quarterback. He doesn't want to open that can of worms today. Mr. Tillman, Nate's Grandfather, doesn't know when to stop. Chuck carries his grandson on the team for one reason only.

Nate can't find his way out of a paper bag, let alone be a quarterback. Chuck tried hard to turn the clumsy kid into a football player. He did this to get next to Keisha Brown. Keisha Brown attended every practice. She usually sat in her folding chair, absorbing the warm weather with her legs crossed, revealing smooth brown thighs and pretty toes polished in hot pink. Her alluring smile made it difficult for Chuck to focus on the kids at every practice. He gave Nate more playing time because of Keisha. Her son served as his chance to get closer to her, so he tolerated Mr. Tillman.

"Mr. Tillman, give me a minute to pack my bag."

"OK, OK, Chuck, take your time. There's no rush," Mr. Tillman taps his right foot in the grass, annoying Chuck. He isn't particularly fond of Mr. Tillman but thinks about Keisha and stays reticent.

"What can I do for you, Mr. Tillman?" Chuck asks, hiding his apparent discontent.

"Have you ever seen your nephew run with a football?" Mr. Tillman asks, trying hard to hold in his enthusiasm. Mr. Tillman is a short, robust man. He has a head full of white hair. He speaks with a lisp, which makes spit fly out of his mouth when he talks.

"David?" Chuck inquires, trying to gather his thoughts while dodging spit.

"Yes, sir, that boy can run. He's a natural," Mr. Tillman's sagging cheeks look like worn leather form into a smile.

"Where did you see David run?" Mr. Tillman can hear the sense of urgency in his tone. He tries to lighten the news.

"The little boys were playing a football game on the next field. Nothing too rough, though. Your nephew ran like somebody was chasing him. No one could tackle him. He even jumped over some kids. You had to see it for yourself," Chuck refuses to hear anymore. He thanks Mr. Tillman for sharing the information and heads toward David. Chuck is fuming. David blatantly disobeyed him. What if his grandmother had come to the field to check on David? He would have no explanation. David was playing with fire, and Chuck would put it out.

David sits nervously on the last row of the faded green bleachers with his sneakers and clothes full of dirt. For the previous ten minutes, David had been seated on the bleachers watching Mr. Tillman talking to his Uncle and suspected the conversation could have been better. A half-hour earlier, Mr. Tillman was the loudest parent cheering on the field when he saw David's running ability. David wondered how long before Mr. Tillman would tell his uncle. Seeing the frown on his uncle's face heading in his direction, he knew Mr. Tillman had spilled the beans.

"David, what were you doing on the other field?" Uncle Chuck asks furiously.

"I was playing with some of my friends," David proclaims in a whisper.

"Talk louder, boy. I can't hear you!" David clears his throat and tries again. "I was playing football with some of my friends," he says louder.

"What did I tell you about playing football, David?" David puts on an innocent face, staring at the ground.

"I was bored, Uncle Chuck. I wanted to have some fun like the rest of the kids."

"David, if you got hurt, that's my ass on the line. I don't need your grandmother coming down on me. You must follow my rules, or I will not let you accompany me anymore."

"But I can play just as good as the kids on your team."

"I don't care what you think you can do in this field. Leave the game to the other children. I bring you with me to help and not to get hurt. One day, when you're bigger, you can play. Until then, you have to follow my rules."

"It's not right, Uncle Chuck," he cries, displaying his unhappiness. Chuck kneels on one knee, making eye contact with David. He lowers his voice, patting David's head.

"I understand, little man. I know how you feel, but give it some more time. I promise I will let you play when the time is right."

"You promise, Uncle Chuck?"

"I promise, but you have to make me a promise."

"What kind of promise?" He wipes his eyes.

"You have to promise me you'll stay off the football field,"
David hugs him.

"I promise no more football."

"That's my boy, now let's go home."

"Can we stop at McDonalds?"

"Aren't you tired of eating McDonalds?"

"No, I can eat McDonalds every day," He smiles. Chuck
gives him a shrewd look. "Not off my money, you won't, but
today I will make an exception."

"Thanks, Uncle Chuck."

The right moment came sooner than David expected. Uncle Chuck
prepared his team for several weeks. A playoff elimination game is
tomorrow. Chuck feels confident his team will do well. The boys know
the plays. Their level of conditioning is adequate, and they are hungry
for a championship. Their hard work will soon display itself on the
field. Today, Chuck decides to take it easy on the kids. It's the last
practice before Friday's big showdown. He tells David to start the roll
call. Everyone responds to their names called except for Chauncey
Holloway, the starting running back who many regard as a man among
boys. Chauncey is only ten but looks fourteen. David walks over to
Chuck.

"Uncle Chuck, Chauncey isn't here."

"He'll be here. He's probably running a little late. Chauncey never
misses a practice. He's the best running back I have. Give him some
more time. Sometimes, his mother works late and rushes to arrive

soon. He has the green light but not the rest of my players. He's earned it."

"Do you want me to fill the cups with water?"

"No, not yet. I will let the kids have fun today and relax before the big game." When Chuck pronounced his last words, Chauncey came hobbling across the field on crutches. Every team member looks dejected. Their hope is lost. Chuck rubs his eyes to make sure his vision isn't deceiving him. As Chauncey gets closer, there is no deception. The crutches are for real, along with a cast on his right foot. How could this happen? Chuck thinks to himself. Not now; the big game is tomorrow.

"Coach, I'm sorry," Chauncey gently speaks.
"What happened? You were fine a couple of days ago."

"I didn't listen to you," Chuck isn't psychic, but he feels what is coming next. He inspects Chauncey's lowered shoulders and pitiful face and immediately recognizes what transpired. Chuck has a simple rule set in place during the football season. No other sports are allowed when playing football for him. The kids can play whatever they choose when the season ends—no ifs, and, or buts about it. A majority of his players disagree with the rule but cooperate with Chuck. His players know their playing time will be over if he finds out. Chauncey deliberately disregarded his it.

"So, what sport were you playing when this happened?"

"I was playing Basketball, and a kid landed on my ankle and fractured it," Chuck looks at Chauncey's cast in disgust. He calls out to the other players standing on the field.
"You see what happens when you refuse to follow my rules? How often have I told each of you not to play any other sport while playing football for me?"

"All the time!" The boys yell in unison, except for Chauncey.

"Chauncey, you're part of this team, right?"

"Yes," he answers dejectedly.

"How many times, Chauncey?"

"All the time. I'm sorry, coach."

"Don't say sorry to me. You owe an apology to your team," Chauncey lifts his head and stares at the grief on their faces. He hops over closer to his team, standing in a circle.

"I'm sorry, guys. I didn't listen, but we still can win."

"And how do you figure that? You're the best running back that we have. Our running game will be over. Yards will be hard to make," Chuck retaliates.

"Not to worry, coach, we have David," the other players join in agreement, hesitantly nodding.

"Oh, everyone has seen David run knowing I didn't want him on the football field and never even told me once? You guys know how to keep a secret, right?" The team remains quiet, looking for Chauncey's leadership.

"Coach, my little brother told me about David. He said David is hard to tackle," David busies himself with the water cooler pretending not to hear. The children gaze in his direction.

"Coach Chuck, just let him run for a few plays. If he fails, we won't mention it again," Chuck takes a deep breath, letting the discomfort dissipate through his lungs. Permitting David to play is challenging to come to terms with. What if David gets injured? How would he explain? He has a tough decision to make, and time is running out.

"David, go put on some equipment. If you get hurt, everything will be over. You better not get hurt. Do you hear me?"

"I won't get hurt. I'm tough."

"You better be, or the courts will be tougher on me." In a flash, David gets dressed. Chuck has second thoughts when David returns fully dressed, but he keeps his word to the team.

"Ok, guys, listen up. I want you to tackle David just as you would anyone else in this field. I want to see if he can run like everyone is telling me. Don't cut him any slack, but don't kill him either. And you guys blocking up front for David, make sure you give him some room to get through the holes. I'm giving David three plays, that's it. If I don't like what I see in three plays, he's removing the equipment."

"Three plays?" Chauncey asks, wanting more.

"Chauncey, it's more than enough. You're lucky he's getting that."

The players take the field, lining up in their offensive and defensive formations. Chuck walks over to the quarterback, giving him three offensive plays to run. After the three plays are over, the team awaits Chuck's answer. In all his years of coaching and playing football as a child, he's never seen anything close to what he just witnessed. David made the defense play like beginners. He ran with such skill, calculating each defender's move and counteracting it with his own. His exceptional speed was no match for anyone on the field.

"David, where did you learn to run like that?" Chuck asks, looking mystified.

"From watching Chauncey, I want to be just like him, Uncle Chuck," David gazes at Chauncey. Chauncey nods approvingly.

"Well, David, you can be like anyone. The way you run."

"Do I run like my dad?"

"Your father never played football. He was too intellectual."

"What's intellectual?"

"In-tel-lec-tual David, it means very smart."

"Did he ever play any sports?"

"Nah, your dad thought sports were a waste of time. And besides, he wasn't the athletic type."

"So, where did I get my speed from?"

"Your guess is as good as mine."

"Maybe I got it from you, Uncle Chuck."

"I was a decent athlete, David, but nothing compared to you." After Chuck inserted David into the lineup, the team was even better without Chauncey. They went on to win three consecutive championships, and not a word of it ever reached David's grandmother. Inside the locker room, Coach Adelman stands in front of his pro team as the chants win or go home gradually diminish. He just turned sixty-five last week but talks like a vibrant young coach. His rosy cheeks and clear gray eyes skim over each player, stopping in David's direction.

"A few more touchdowns, David, and we can put this game out of reach. I was expecting more of a challenge from the BC Lions. I don't know why they're favored to win. Their defense isn't that great. When you guys hit the field in the second half, give them hell. I want to end this game early and prove we belong here." Coach Adelman completes his brief speech, making his way out of the locker room.

"Oh, David, I almost forgot. You have a phone call. Make it quick; we're on the field in ten minutes."

"From who?"

"Your uncle," David leaves the locker, heading straight for Coach Adelman's office. His secretary hands David the phone.

"Hello?"

"You're playing a great game, David. I'm proud of you, boy. I taught you a lot, didn't I?" He sounds drunk, slurring his words.

"Yeah, you sure did, but I don't have much time to talk unc. What's up?"

"I just want to tell you something I haven't told anyone yet. You're like my son. I think you should be the first to know."

"Know what?"

"Maybe I shouldn't tell you now. It might distract you from your game."

"Uncle Chuck, tell me now." I want to know what's wrong."

"I'll tell you later, David. Just take care of business on the field."

"Are you sure?"

"I'm positive. After you win, call me."

"I will certainly do that. Make sure you answer the phone. You hear me?"

"Yes, boy, I hear you."

"Alright, I have to go. I'll call you later."

"David?"

"Yes."

"I love you."

"I love you too, unc."

"Is everything okay, David?" The slender African-American secretary asks.

"Everything's fine," he answers in distress. He quickly heads back to the locker room, thinking about his uncle. His uncle became drunk when he was depressed. He usually has a few beers occasionally, but not enough to develop intoxication. The last time he was this drunk, his job laid him off. David worries about his uncle. The one genuine family member he has left. David will check on his uncle as soon as the game is over. As David walks onto the field, he stops to relish the moment. Filled are the seats in the arena. One dedicated fan has David's Jersey number painted on his bare chest. The Canadian locals are serious about their football. When David entered the NFL draft, many teams passed him over. Their reasoning for not drafting David was related to the college he played for. The NFL teams informed David his touchdown runs and record-breaking yards came against mediocre schools in his division.

David didn't let that stop him from pursuing other options. He surprised his fans and uncle when he signed with the Montreal Alouettes. His salary is close to three hundred thousand dollars a year. The NFL wants a piece of David and will give him much more money than the CFL. Over the past several years, the loyal CFL fans and Montreal Alouettes organization have treated David like one of their own. The switch from the States to Canada was initially tricky, but David adjusted like other players who had transitioned before him. More than half the population in Montreal speaks French. All street signs and public notices are in French, which required David to learn critical phrases before arriving in Montreal.

The start of the second half isn't going as smoothly as the first. In the first half, the Montreal Alouettes seemed to be playing football without any resistance from their opposition. The BC Lions play football like a different team in the second half. David is having trouble gaining yards, and his quarterback is sacked several times in the first three minutes of the half. The BC Lions have tied the game with two third-quarter interceptions leading to touchdowns. Coach Adelman calls for a time-out on the field. He gathers his team together in a huddle. "Look, I don't care what we did in the first half. We have to play better football this quarter. We worked hard to get here. Stop playing like a bunch of kids. I want to win this game. So go back out there and leave everything on the field. David, the first two plays are going to you. Do what you do best."

"It's taken care of coach."

The stadium noise sounds like thunder. David tunes out the noise, focusing on the task at hand. "Forty-two option sweep," the quarterback calls inside the huddle. This play is by far David's favorite. He usually scores easily with three offensive linemen in front to clear his path. A touchdown at this point will give the Allottees the go-ahead lead. Football is David's elixir. When things in his personal life aren't going so swell, football eases the pain. He feels like a God on the field, omnipotent and perfect. Football removes the bitterness he lives with from his parent's death and the untimely heart attack his grandmother suffered.

Furthermore, football aided him during his youth by removing the pain he constantly endured at the group home from racial slurs inflicted upon his mixed heritage. David stands as the single halfback in the backfield. The opposing team has everyone on the front line preparing for the run except for the lone safety. The center snaps the ball into the quarterback's hands. David quickly breaks to the outside, where he can receive the ball with three blockers up front. What happens next, David faintly remembers. The three linemen fail their assignments miserably, leaving David vulnerable. Lineman number one is stopped in his tracks before David receives the ball. The second lineman pulls left instead of right where the play is developing, and too many defenders overcome the third lineman. David tries to dodge each defender. He spins and shakes a couple of linebackers. David creates an open space in the center of the field. He starts to pull away from his adversaries. The safety is waiting in the middle of the area. David tries to maneuver around him. His attempt is unsuccessful. The safety latches onto his left leg, slowing him down. David spins right, then left to shake him. He is almost free. Within seconds, he is blindsided helmet to helmet from behind and collapses. A penalty flag reaches the air. The fans hold their breaths. The training staff rushes to his aide. Before moving him, the trainers check for broken bones. They carefully turn him over on his back and remove his helmet.

"David, are you okay?" Coach Adelman asks.

"I feel so much pain. It feels like a knife is stabbing me repeatedly inside my head. Can you take off my helmet so I can breathe? I don't have any strength," The trainers and Coach Adelman look at each other perplexed.

"David, your helmet has been off for ten minutes."

"Then why is it so dark, Coach?" Coach Adelman clutches David's hand, moving in closer to his face.

"David, can you see me?"

"No, I can't see anything."

CHAPTER 16

PAUL:

I don't know how long I was asleep, but I feel like a new person. My heart rate is back to normal. The swirling dizziness has disappeared, and the sweat has ceased. I turn to look at the doctor to tell him I can now finish my story.

"By the way, Doc, how long was I asleep?"

"I say thirty minutes."

"Well, I feel great."

"Paul, we can continue this at another session. I realize you need more time to progress. We can gradually make things better in smaller increments. I believe this will be the best thing for you." I'm ready to tell my story, and he wants me to stop. He needs to make up his mind. I have to continue. The only way to get Patricia out of my head is to keep talking. I have to let her go. She will not control my life forever.

"I would like to finish. Let's get this over with," the doctor said, fingers tracing the scar on his face. Can I ask you something?"

"Certainly, what would you like to know?" His bulging eyes grow more significant.

"Your scar, how did it happen?" He does not answer me right away. He sits stationary, trying to gather his thoughts together. His scowl informs me I just hit a nerve. I should've kept my mouth shut. I feel ashamed for asking. I turn my head back around, hoping he's not too upset.

"Paul, you seem a bit worried; not to worry, I get asked this question a lot," he withdraws his grimace. I would prefer to discuss it another time. For now, let's continue," I feel a small amount of relief.

"On Sunday mornings before service begins, my routine seldom changes. I shower. I have a bowl of oatmeal and then put on my clothes. I usually retrieve the Sunday morning paper off the front lawn, but I ran late. I would have known what was in store if I had read the article. I backed my Nissan Altima out of the driveway, heading for church. Center Street was silent. A striking serenity ran through my melting-pot neighborhood like quietness before the storm. The colonial-style condominiums mirror each other in comparison. They are brown, white, yellow, and identical to the makeup of the multiethnic neighbors living there. Each unit has a sweeping driveway leading into a vast two-car garage. Adjacent to the driveway, planted in rich soil, sits green bayberry shrubs with delicate textured foliage and an interesting branch structure decorating the front lawn. The private thirty-six hundred square feet units resemble a miniature movie studio. Exquisite rooftops cover diverse rooms seen through eye-catching design windows. I am blessed to be able to live in an area as nice as this one, but we have our problems just like any other neighborhood in America. Halfway through the block, I noticed something extraordinary. Dan Murphy, a chunky Irishman with black hair and thick bifocal glasses who lives at the end of the street, waved to me, smiling as I passed him. To the average person, his gesture would seem normal. But you see, I've lived there for three years, and Dan has never uttered two words to me since moving into the neighborhood. It bemused me so much that I veered close to the sidewalk, scraping my tire against the curb."

"So, Dan hated you, I presume?"

"I don't know if he hated me, but he never showed me anything otherwise. I've tried to break the ice, but he always ignored me. I found his gesture very odd that morning. He seemed to be laughing, almost ridiculing me. About five minutes away from the church, Oliver flags me down."

"Who's Oliver?"

"Oliver is a homeless man and dresses better than most people I know. He has dry salt and peppered hair, brown eyes, dark skin, and is thin as a rail. When I saw Oliver, he wore black slacks, a white shirt buttoned to the top, white shoes, and a white belt. Everyone knows him. He begs for money, asking anyone for a handout. I've frequently made donations to him in the past. He's usually holding up a cardboard sign. On this particular Sunday, the sign read I will work for food as long as you can cook."

"Paul, that's the funniest thing I've ever heard," the doctor starts laughing hysterically. He cannot stop laughing.

"Do you want me to give you a few minutes, doctor?" I ask, laughing along with him.

"I'm okay," he says, placing his hand over his mouth. "Please continue."

"When I reach in my pocket to give Oliver another handout, he says he doesn't want the money. I then asked him what changed. He tells me I've been so good to him over the years, and I will probably need more money than him. Before walking away from me, he says God bless you with a concerned face because you will need him. Oliver's actions scare me more than anything. He never passes up money. I know this for a fact. Saint Luke's church is on State Street in New Haven, CT. The church resides in the business district but is accessible to everyone. Even persons living in the city without reliable transportation can ride the city bus, which stops directly in front of the building. Founded in 1923, Saint Luke's has served the community for eighty-nine years. It resembles a traditional church building. Saint Luke's architecture captures the shape of a cross with its pointy dome protracting toward the sky. The facility conveniently seats three thousand people. I became the head minister after pastor Raymond Johnson retired. I sat under his wing for a year to learn the day-to-day operations before taking over. As I got closer to the church, traffic was at a standstill. It seemed unusual to me. Typically, there isn't any traffic at 9:15 a.m. I must have sat in traffic for 10 minutes before deciding to park my vehicle two blocks away and walk. Church started at 9:30. I had five minutes to get there. I quickened my pace to make it on time. Fifty feet from the church, I couldn't believe what I witnessed. Chaos surrounded Saint Luke, not only by the police but the entire congregation, three news trucks, local reporters, and bystanders who wanted to know what was happening. A sea of pictures covers the building from front to rear. From where I stood, I couldn't identify the images. Mr. Earl Thomas, the church custodian, is working hard at trying to take the pictures down. The crowd becomes ecstatic. They began to push through the police barricade, causing a free-for-all. Several from the eager mob squeeze through the barrier, grabbing photos while others are detained and told to go home by police. The news crews were filming it all as reporters commented on the scene. I had to find out what was happening. I ran as fast as I could. I accidentally collided with a small, light-skinned boy running from the church. I reached down to help him up. He looked up at me, frightened. He got back to his feet. He ran so fast that his photo fell out of his back pocket. In haste, I picked up the image. The child had neatly rolled the picture together. It looked more like a scroll than a picture. I carefully separated the ends with both hands, opening the photo. The photo conveyed pain and torture. It made my stomach turn inside. In the picture, Patricia Martin was nude, badly beaten in her bedroom, and blood covered her body. Her right eye is partially closed. Her nose looks broken. She wrote, Paul Mitchell did this to me in big, bold letters at the bottom of the picture. He raped me, beat me, and tried to take my life, but I managed to escape his attack. Paul is the devil, not a man of God. He's deceitful, do not trust him. Her words hurt. I was overwhelmed by her false accusations. How in God's name could she say these things about me? She was trying to destroy my image and career with this horrid picture."

"So, this led you to attempt suicide?"

"Not entirely. The last months before arriving here have been dreadful. The church elders have plotted against me and accused me of stealing money from the treasury. People don't like change. When I took over the church, I made many changes right away, and it pressured the board members to slander my name. Each day, the board came up with different schemes to get rid of me. A few teenage girls singing in the choir have falsely accused me of touching them inappropriately. I know for a fact the girls were coerced. More than half of the girls singing in the choir have parents on the board of trustees. The false claims are under investigation. I found out later they interviewed a few pastors without my knowledge. With everything going against me, they can finally get rid of me for good. Before this thing with Patricia happened, someone broke into my home several times, destroying my clothing and furniture, and spray painted every wall in my home black. The person or persons confiscated my credit cards. The creditors are harassing me to pay back the stolen credit cards. A man has a breaking point."

"Why didn't you try to clear your name of these false accusations regarding Patricia?"

"Evidence was stacked against me. I didn't have a way out. I guess I panicked."

"Paul, do you remember who saved your life?" His voice sounds peaceful, almost hypnotic. *I wish the man on that warm, foggy night hadn't convinced me not to jump off the Brooklyn Bridge. I didn't want to live anymore, but he insisted I had much more to do.*

"I remember him saving me, but he should have let me jump. I don't recall how he reached me. He just appeared out of nowhere, like from a cloud. It was something about him that made me forget my troubles. When he spoke to me, the weight on my shoulders instantly lifted. My spirit felt reborn. There wasn't anything special about his character. He wore ordinary blue jeans, white Nikes, a New York Giant's jersey, and a Giant's cap. The caramel manner of his skin was flawless. His face expressed an aura of extreme happiness. There was something strange about his eyes. When I looked into his eyes, I saw my reflection."

"Like a mirror, Paul?"

"Yes and no. I saw images surrounding me."

"What kind of images, Paul?"

"There were two different images in two different directions. The first image was north of me. It was an image of my father with people surrounding him. One person would leave his chamber, and another would appear. He wrote down their names in a dense black book. The people seemed never to stop coming in as my father tirelessly recorded their names."

"Can you describe some of the people surrounding him?"

"Ordinary working-class people, there was nothing unusual about them."

"What were the people saying to your father?"

"The people weren't saying anything. The room was silent, and no one said a word."

"How did this image make you feel?"

"I felt my father's desire to help people. He did whatever it took to help a lost soul. His undying pledge to serve man touched my heart in a way I've never experienced before. After that, the image disappeared."

"Could this man and the image you saw have been fabricated on your part? Sometimes, when we are not ourselves, stressful events can conjure thoughts from our subconscious and begin to take control of our thoughts, including voices." *He thinks I'm completely insane. I may have attempted suicide, but I know what I saw.*

"Remember, I'm a Minister. One thing I always try to do, whether right or wrong, is to tell the truth."

"Several reports were stating you were screaming uncontrollably when the police pulled you down off the bridge. A few witnesses reported you were alone on the bridge. Tell me exactly how you were able to see an image while attempting suicide?" *I'm beginning to lose my patience. His attitude is frustrating me. He's speaking to me as one of his third-floor subjects. He's being insensitive to my explanation. I'm sure his therapy sessions are high in number. I'm just another crazy person to him.*

"Do you believe in God, doctor?" *Again, I turn my head around, looking for an answer. He narrows his eyes slightly, making them appear smaller. Running his long fingers through my folder, he pauses before speaking.*

"Mr. Mitchell, my faith is irrelevant at this time. I'm here to understand the what, when, where, why, and how of your decision. My main concern is what you did when you saw the first image?" *I guess that means no. What does he think I was doing, playing with my fingers and toes? I was trying to end my life by jumping into the abyss and alleviating my misery.* "How can a pastor give up so easily after saving so many lost souls?" *Who is he to judge me?*

"You would never understand the life of a minister and how the public judges us. The church crucifies us to the full extent along with the public."

"He without sin let him cast the first stone. Those are Christ's exact words. Am I right, reverend?"

"Those are the words of God, but not of God's people." *You included.* People desire blood with your head on a silver platter. Watching someone suffer is entertainment for people. Society thrives by exploiting the plight of its citizens. Controversy makes money. The media runs with the story, initiating everyone to chase after it, and then media frenzy develops."

"Paul, I think we should continue tomorrow. It's late, and we both need our rest."

"I will rest when I'm dead. I would like to get this off of my chest. You got me started, so don't interrupt me now. Please let me finish, I beg you."

"Five minutes, and that's final."

"Thank you."

"A second image appeared from the south direction. Again, it was my father. In this second image, he is talking to a man, the very same man who stood next to me on the bridge. He told my father not to become discouraged and continue to help people. I sensed my father's burden. His heart was troubled, and the conversation with the angel renewed his strength. The vision ends."

"Paul, it's been five months since your arrival. When you first began your therapy sessions, it was difficult to articulate. I see more progression, but we still have to take one session at a time to cure you ultimately. The medicine is an important part of your recovery. A lot has happened to you in the past few months. For this to work, I recommend therapy, medicine, and time to heal from your traumatic events. Get some rest. We will talk more tomorrow."

The outside temperature is twenty-five degrees, but the wind chill makes it feel ten degrees colder. If you are indoors looking outside, the bright sunlight may fool you into believing otherwise. Patricia's bedroom is dark. The white Venetian blinds are tightly closed. Her brownish-yellow curtains cover any space where light may enter the room. Patricia Martin sits in front of her mahogany mirrored dresser, somewhat satisfied. Her scheme worked just the way she planned it. She must finish the job. Paul must die. The police are taking their sweet time waiting for Paul's release from a mental institution before questioning him. She wants him sentenced right away. Twenty years of jail time is the correct number for her. A man of his importance would not survive. He tried to take his life once. The prison will surely bring him over the edge. What if a jury of his peers finds him innocent? She worries. What if the detectives mishandle the evidence? She cannot wait around for this outcome. She must act fast. Paul doesn't deserve to recover. Patricia stares back at her reflection. The scars and bruises have almost healed. She hired a couple of guys to work her over and take the pictures afterward to show the world what Paul had done. One of the dumb brutes lost control, nearly causing permanent damage to her right eye. She almost shot him but thought twice about the consequences. There is still a trace of blood inside her retina, the fool. He will pay later. She must take care of Paul first, and she knows exactly how to do it.

CHAPTER 17

CHINA

"China, how long will you stay in this house?"

"Does it matter? No one cares about me anyway. The world is doing just fine without me."

"That's not true. You have devoted fans dying to see you. They miss your voice."

"Kelly, I have no one but you, but eventually, you will leave me like Mark and the rest of my fans. When the money stops coming in, you will walk away too," her remark startles Kelly.

"How dare you say that to me? I've been with you from the beginning when you didn't have a dime or a name. I fronted the money to get you started. I paid for your clothing and transported you around the world. It has taken years for you to reach this level of success. You started from the bottom, and I provided a solid foundation to help you reach the top," Kelly pauses, taking a deep breath, then exhales. I'm like your second mother. I've taught you so many things about the music industry. You're more than money to me. I see you as the daughter I never had. Money is short-term. Love is endless, and don't you ever forget it?"

"I can't even stand on my own two feet. I'm helpless without this wheelchair. Just get out, Kelly. Get out of my house! Manage someone who isn't crippled. Go get money from them because you made a lot from me," her offensive words pierce through Kelly's heart. She fights hard to hold back the tears.

"Oh, this is what you've become, a bitter woman giving up and feeling sorry for yourself? I will not manage anyone else. I'm here to stay whether you like it or not. I never would've thought it. You, of all people, quit something you've been passionate about since childhood. What will you do? This mansion costs money to live in. What about your luxurious cars in your garage, your chef, your expensive taste for the finer things, and your endorsement deals? Do you think you can afford these things if you don't perform?" China rolls her wheelchair quietly toward her double glass doors. She looks out over the acres of land she possesses. When the real estate agent first presented the mansion to her some years ago, she adored the property. She loves the spacious high ceilings along with the smooth marble wood floors. In the center of the living room, wrapped together in a circle leading to ten bedrooms, is a beautifully adorned set of stairs with railings made of gold. The massive symmetrical brownstone front exterior makes the house appear impenetrable. The mansion is by far a sheer masterpiece. She wondered how long she would have to sell it.

"I've already lost my endorsements. The companies didn't even have the decency to tell me in person. In three weeks, I've received three separate letters from Maybelline, Infiniti, and Victoria Secret canceling my endorsement deals," Kelly walks over to China, placing her hand on her shoulder.

"How can they get away with treating you like a common criminal? I will see to it they pay for this. We'll sue them," Kelly responds angrily.

"There's nothing we can do, Kelly. It's in the contract. If an artist can't perform, the contract is void; it's as simple as that."

"Then you have to perform China. Your legs aren't strong enough to stand, but your voice is still mighty. You can't give up China. Just have a little faith," Kelly pleads.

"Faith, don't talk to me about faith! I've heard it my entire life. My mother ensured it, and do you know what she did to me? She locked me in a small studio apartment while she got drunk and God knows what else. She took me away from my father, friends, and my childhood. Oh, Miss Sanctified Henrietta only thought about her. So, like I commanded before, get out of my house now. I don't need you anymore."

"Who do you think you are to boss me around? I promoted you well, and this is how you repay me?"

"My voice promoted me. I would've made it with whoever managed me," tears well up in Kelly's eyes.

"China, I know you don't mean this. I know you are hurting inside, but we can get through this together. Please don't give up."

"Did you hear me, Kelly? I said to get out and don't ever come back. I will manage myself. I don't need anyone to help me. I've been doing it all my life," China's gaze remains on her lawn. When the door slams, China closes her eyes. *What have I done?* China guided her wheelchair along the newly designed ramp installed when she lost usage in both legs. As she reaches the top of the ramp, she strolls to her bedroom and stops at the foot of the bed. She strains to lift herself from the wheelchair. With ample struggle, she throws herself onto the bed and cries.

Thanks for reading my story, A Second Chance Part 1. Parts 2 and 3 are now available. Happy reading!

Don't miss out!

Visit the website below and you can sign up to receive emails whenever Edmond White publishes a new book. There's no charge and no obligation.

https://books2read.com/r/B-A-DMSDB-OWKWC

BOOKS 2 READ

Connecting independent readers to independent writers.